BRASS, UNLEASHED!

Down below the murk, Brass, in the shape of a great beast, nuzzled himself lethargically into the ooze at the bottom of the bay. He swallowed down one last chunk of the man flesh, and he felt good. He had only begun to make up for all those centuries, all that seemingly endless wait, the suffering, the anguish, the dreadful loneliness. He would wait yet awhile. There were still more people out there on the beach. They were not like any people he had ever seen before, but he was not surprised at that. Had he not watched life forms change beneath the sea? And they had those strange, new, large animals that growled so fiercely. He had waited an eternity down there. He could wait a little longer.

BRASS

ROBERT J. CONLEY

LEISURE BOOKS   NEW YORK CITY

A LEISURE BOOK®

April 1999

Published by

Dorchester Publishing Co., Inc.
276 Fifth Avenue
New York, NY 10001

ISBN 0-8439-4505-2

BRASS

Preface

He lolled his head slightly to the left just to create some distracting stir around himself. The stale water was intolerably still, and he felt the urge to cause something, however small, to happen to relieve the overwhelming sense of boredom. The pain had long since ceased. Long ago he had thought that the pain was too much to be borne, but it had stopped, and he was bored. Even a return of the pain would have been a welcome relief.

He had no idea how long he had lain there. A hundred years? A thousand? Ten thousand? He had forgotten ages past what it was like to walk on the surface of the earth, what it was like to breathe fresh air, what the rocks and hills and trees looked like. He longed for the world of the surface, which for him no longer existed, and the longing had become a dull ache that had replaced the sharp pain in his chest—the pain that had slowly faded away.

For a while—how long was a while? A few hundred years? He couldn't say, but for a while he had experienced relief from the boredom when he felt small things crawling between his toes and nestling into the hair of his armpits and his crotch. Now he imagined that he could actually feel the barnacles growing on his wide, once smooth forehead. Time for him had become so slow that it had almost ceased to move in its vast circle. He could feel the slow growth of his own hair and nails, but not even these slight tickling sensations could any longer amuse him. He hardly noticed them anymore.

Of course, life went on around him: life-forms large and small floated past, occasionally even brushed against his nearly motionless, out-stretched, alien form. Now and then some un-suspecting, unfortunate thing small enough to do so even wandered into his open, eager, wait-ing mouth, and then he would crunch it. These too rare moments in his nearly private eternity of timelessness, his endless dull ache of existence, were just about the only pleasure left to him and the only means he had of attempting to satisfy his constant, gnawing hunger.

At first, when he had still felt pain, when he had struggled violently against the vines that bound his arms and legs and against the thing that pinned him down and caused the terrible pain in his chest, the life-forms had been many and varied, but, of course, his violent flailings, wrenchings, and jerkings, and his gurgling howls, had driven them away from him.

When he had finally given up the struggle, when the pain had gone away, when the vines had dropped away due to age or erosion or the nibblings of tiny anonymous things, he saw to his dismay that there were fewer live things around—fewer in total numbers and fewer in kind. Then he noticed that some of them were new. There were species of life he had not known before, so he knew that time went on and that the world around him changed. He wondered how it might have changed above.

He felt something crawling up his jaw. It was moving toward his mouth. He desperately fought his impatience, his sense of urgency, and he slowly, almost imperceptibly, opened his cavernous mouth. He felt the thing creep onto his lower lip and touch his tongue, and he lay perfectly still. If he bit too soon, he might not get it all. He waited, and he felt it crawl on in, and then he clamped his teeth and pressed his lips tightly together. He had it.

The thing turned, frantically, he thought with delight, upon his tongue, looking for a way out of the trap. It lashed its tiny body around in its confusion and panic. He didn't bite it right away, for that would have brought an end to the episode much too soon. He let it crawl around his teeth and tickle the roof of his mouth, and he felt intense pleasure at such a tiny blessing.

At last he tired of the game, and the signals from his stomach nagged at him with growing persistence, and so he swallowed down the thing and felt it tickle all the way along the path of his gullet and for a short while inside his stomach. Then the enzymes and the acids did their job and killed it in the process of digesting, and he was bored again.

Then he saw the day. There was a cloudless sky at sunrise, and he could see not only to the surface but through it and beyond. He could see the end of the pole thrusting itself obscenely into the open air, and, yes, he could see the wretched crows, the two of them, perched upon its end. Here was something he could do.

Slowly he raised his arms and legs and let them fall to one side. Then he swung them all with all his weight to the other side and back again. Soon he picked up some momentum, and he was flailing around there on his back violently, lurching, jerking, causing the pole to rock and shake. High above, the crows were startled from their perch. They danced around, not wanting to abandon their station. They berated him loudly and vociferously with their harsh caws. He reveled in their extreme agitation and their frantic worry, and the sounds they made, sounds that were much distorted before they reached him where he lay, were music to his ears. He laughed, and his laughter made an ugly, gurgling vibration that sent bubbles rising from his mouth.

Soon he tired, he lay still again, the waters calmed, the pole stopped trembling, and the crows perched down again upon its top. The deadly, boring silence reigned, and he wondered once again how much longer he must wait until the end of Time, until the day the world would die. He knew that he, himself, could not die alone, for he was not blessed with mortality. As long as the earth lived, so must he. He stared upward along the length of the pole, his eyes not blinking, and he longed for the death of the world and for his own welcome release into the Darkening Land.

Chapter One

The stretch of beach was an eyesore, one of
those man-made blights on the natural beauty
of the landscape that are so much a part of the
twentieth century. It was a small bay or inlet,
the mouth of which had become partially but
effectively dammed by a gathering of debris co-
operating with the natural movement of the
ocean's floor caused by the ebb and flow of the
tide, so that even when the tide receded, there
remained a pool of increasingly slimy and stag-
nant salt water dotted with pieces of assorted
junk.

BRASS

The beach itself was shallow; it was stopped short by an eroding cliff that outlined the inlet. The burned-out bodies of two old cars lay on the beach, along with a collection of worn-out and discarded tires. Along the rim, houses had been built to overlook the ocean, but some years past, the crumbling of the cliff had moved its edge dangerously close to the dwellings. One house had a corner protruding precariously over the edge.

The entire housing development had been condemned and, along with a long stretch of the beach below, had been enclosed in a ten-foot-high chain-link fence. Signs posted at regular intervals along the fence marked the area as dangerous and off-limits to unauthorized people. Evidence of vandalism to the houses and the ever-increasing trash heap below provided proof that the signs had not been effective.

Out in the water within wading distance at low tide (if anyone had been brave or foolish enough to wade into that vile and putrid pool) stood a lone, long-weathered pole, in appearance about the diameter of a telephone pole at its topmost end but seeming to taper gradually where it disappeared into the water. On top of the pole sat two haggard crows.

As the crowd gathered on the beach in a spot that had been partially cleared to allow for the gathering, the crows began to scold. When the crowd not only failed to disperse but instead continued to grow, the scolding became louder and harsher. The crows seemed to take turns flying up and toward the crowd, then back to the pole. They were largely ignored by the humans. A man stepped out in front of the crowd, his back to the water. He held his hands up over his head.

"Ladies and gentlemen," he shouted, "may I have your attention, please?"

The noise of the crowd subsided into a low and innocuous murmur. The man spoke over it.

"I give you our mayor," he said, "the Honorable Samuel B. Purchase."

There was applause and cheering as the mayor stepped up onto the end of a conveniently placed empty wire-rope reel. He smiled and nodded in response to the crowd.

"Thank you," he said. "Thank you, friends and neighbors and fellow citizens. Thank you."

He cleared his throat loudly and pompously, reached into his hip pocket for a handkerchief, and mopped his sweating brow, which sloped down from a far receding hairline. The sun was high overhead and beat down relentlessly on the littered beach.

"We're here for the official announcement," the mayor said, "of something you all know about already, or else you wouldn't be here in the first place."

Mayor Purchase laughed a little at what he fancied to be a clever little joke, and the crowd, taking its cue, chuckled politely, then waited for him to continue.

"This here eyesore," he said, "this garbage dump that we are standing in the middle of, is going to become our own public recreation area. It's going to be a beautiful beach, thanks to the efforts on our behalf of our own congressman, Jeff D. Brower, and I'm not going to steal any more of his thunder. I'm going to get down from here and let him tell you all about it. Give him a big hand, folks. Congressman Brower."

During the ensuing applause, the young man who had initially hushed the crowd stepped up to the reel to give the mayor a hand down. Purchase stepped off the reel, then stepped back to make room for the congressman, his left foot going into the slimy water.

"Damn," he said, jerking his foot out of the water. He could feel the vile liquid sloshing inside his shoe, and he looked down to see a thin, green scum stretched across the shoestrings. Brower, with the assistance of the steadying arm of the young man, climbed up onto the reel.

"Thank you, Oliver," he said.

The applause died down.

"And thank you, Mr. Mayor," he continued.

"It's always a pleasure to get back home and visit with the good people who put me in my congressional seat. But it's a special pleasure today, believe me, my friends, because this is a special day for all of us here. We are going to have our beach."

A roar of pleasure and appreciation rose up from the cheerful crowd. Congressman Brower held up his hands for silence, and the reel tipped slightly to one side, almost causing him to topple into the nasty beach sand. Oliver saved the day.

"Thank you, Oliver," said Brower. "Yes, my friends, the project has been approved, the appropriation has been made, the project engineer is here with me today, and work will begin immediately."

The crowd again made known its pleasure.

"And now, my friends," intoned the congressman, "I want to introduce to you the man who's going to make it all happen. I want you folks to get to know this man and make him feel at home in our community, because he's going to be a part of this community now for a while. The project engineer from the U.S. Army Corps of Engineers in charge of cleaning up and renovating our beach and creating our new community recreational facility, Mr. Joe Shelby."

The crowd began to applaud, and the congressman stepped awkwardly down from the wire-rope reel, assisted, of course, by Oliver. Joe Shelby, standing in the front of the crowd with his wife beside him and facing the congressman, stepped forward, turned slightly to partially face the crowd, and waved his right hand. He was a man in his mid-fifties with a full head of gray hair, a body still vigorous and energetic, and lively eyes. The congressman stepped toward him and took him by the arm.

"Come on, Joe," he said. "Let the people see you."

He pulled Shelby up to the reel, where Shelby turned to face the crowd and waved again.

"Get on up there, Joe," said the congressman.

"No," said Shelby. "I don't need to climb up on that thing."

Mayor Purchase stepped forward to offer reinforcement to the congressman.

"Get up there and talk to the people, Joe," he said. "This is no time for false modesty."

Shelby soon found himself standing on the reel and overlooking the crowd. He felt foolish. He had come to this place to do a job, and he didn't figure that making speeches and acting the fool in front of crowds was a part of that job. Leave that to the politicians. But he was stuck this time. No way out.

"Well," he said, scratching his head, "I, uh, I don't really have much to say. It's, uh, it's all been said, I think, by the mayor and the congressman here. Me and my men, we're ready to go to work, and, uh, when we get done here, we think you'll have yourselves a beach that you'll all be proud of and you'll all enjoy for a long time to come."

There was a smattering of applause, and the congressman's voice boomed out over it.

"Tell them what you're going to do, Joe," he roared. "They'd like to hear that."

Damn that motormouth, Shelby thought. *I wish he'd shut the hell up*. He cleared his throat nervously. He wanted to jump down off the reel and get away from all these people.

"Well," he said, "the plans are right up in your mayor's office, and, uh, I'm sure that you can all go up there and take a look at them just about anytime. That right, Mr. Mayor?"

"Anytime," said Purchase.

"But, uh, what we'll do is, me and my crew, we'll come in here first and just clean up the place. We'll rake up all this trash and haul it out of here, and that includes those condemned houses up there on the shelf and all that chain-link fencing around them. We've got to tear all those down and haul them off.

"Then, well, then we've got to go out there in the water and clean out whatever it is that's holding in this pool here whenever the tide rolls out. Once we've done that, why, pretty soon nature will just take her course, and you'll have clean water here.

"We'll deepen this beach here, and when we cut back the shelf there, we'll build a solid retaining wall so there won't be any more crumbling like you see here. That cliff will stay where we put it, and up on top, you'll have a nice, large, paved parking lot. The beach down here will be all clean sand. Well, there's, uh, there's a little more to it than that, I guess, but that gives you the general picture. You, uh, you can take a look at the drawings in the mayor's office."

Before either Brower or Purchase could think of anything else to tell him to tell the crowd, Shelby jumped down off the reel and hurried back to the side of his wife there at the head of the crowd. She put a hand on his shoulder.

"You did just fine, Joe," she said.

"Yeah," he said. "Hell, I think I'll run for office. Take the mayor's job away from him. Maybe Brower's seat."

"Oh, Joe," she said.

There was a slight lull in the proceedings, a brief moment of indecision, and into the unexpected silence came the angry caws of the crows. The two black birds on the post out in the brackish water were suddenly so loud and so persistent that every head turned to look at them. They seemed to be deliberately scolding the people. Trying his best to ignore them, the mayor, with the help of Oliver, climbed back up onto the reel.

"All right, folks," he said.

The birds barked loudly at his back.

"We're all through down here for now."

Ka, ka, ka, came the cries of the crows. Mayor Purchase glanced over his shoulder at the angry birds and almost lost his balance. He harrumphed and regained his composure.

"Mr. Shelby," he continued, "has asked that we not come back down here and get in the way again after today, not until the work's all done and we have the big, official grand opening."

Ka, ka.

"So let's all move carefully back up the path and on out of here," the mayor said. "We'll gather at my office, out front, and I'll bring out the pictures and the plans, and we'll hold the press conference up there."

Ka, ka, ka.

His heart pounded in anticipation. Something was happening out there. He could tell. He knew it and he felt it. He thought that he heard, ever so faintly, the sound of human voices. He couldn't tell what they were saying, couldn't even be really sure that they were human voices, but there had been something, something unfamiliar to him for a long time, yet something somehow still familiar from a dimly recalled past, something—human. Something not so far away.

And whatever it was, it had angered the crows. He liked that. He could not remember the crows being so angry, so loud, so animated at any time in the timeless time they had spent atop his pole—*his pole*. He growled at himself in anger for the phrase, and the bubbles shot out from between his lips. *His pole*. He had not asked for the pole. He did not want the pole. He hated the pole. He could not recall such anger from the crows except when he had thrashed around to shake the pole. And this time he had been quite still. Something was up. Something had alarmed them. What was it? What could it be? The end of the world?

Mayor Purchase came out of his office and stood at the top of the stairs. The crowd had gathered below. Oliver propped the drawings against the wall on either side of the mayor for all to see.

"There they are, folks," said Purchase. "Plans and drawings. Just as soon as we get this press conference over with, any of you who want to get a closer look can just come right on up here and take all the time you want. Right now I believe we got some gentlemen of the press with their notepads out and waiting.

"Congressman, would you and Mr. Shelby join me up here, please? Some of these questions might be directed at one of you gentlemen. Thank you."

Brower and Shelby moved one to each side of the mayor on the step just below the one on which he stood. Oliver looked over the crowd and pointed a finger at a reporter.

"Mr. Shelby," said the reporter, "just exactly when will work begin?"

"Just exactly the first thing Monday morning," said Shelby. "All the equipment and all the men will be here by then, and we'll get right to work."

"How long will it take and what's the cost?"

"It's about a nine-month and two-and-a-half-million-dollar job," Shelby said.

Another reporter nudged his way to the front of the crowd, and Oliver gave him a nod.

"Congressman Brower," the reporter said, "you've been accused in Washington of sneaking this two-and-a-half-million-dollar appropriation through as a rider on the major highway construction bill. This has been called a classic pork-barrel project. How do you respond to that?"

"If you want to call it sneaking and label it pork barrel," the congressman said, "you just go right on ahead and call it that, sonny. All I know is that the good people of this community wanted that dangerous and ugly beach cleaned up, and they wanted a safe, clean place to go with their families for good, clean, wholesome recreation. They came to me for help, and I got the job done."

The reporters took their notes, a couple of cameras clicked, and a cheer went up from the crowd. Brower hooked his thumbs behind his coat lapels and smiled.

"Mr. Shelby," shouted another reporter, not waiting to be called on, "has the Corps of Engineers done an environmental-impact study?"

"The study was done. Yeah," said Shelby. "It was done and submitted through the proper channels, approved, and is now on file. It's a matter of public record."

"If you news boys had done your homework before you came down here this morning," said the mayor, "you wouldn't be needing to ask some of these questions, now would you? We held a series of public hearings right here in our town hall. Everything's been done strictly according to the law. All proper procedures have been followed. Everything is open and aboveboard, and I don't see any point to any more of those kinds of questions. Let's not stir up any controversy here over nothing. Let's keep this friendly. All right?"

"Mr. Mayor—"

"I think we're about done here," said Purchase. "Thank you for coming, folks. Oliver, take those drawings back inside. We'll see all of you later at the big, grand opening. Bye, now."

Purchase went inside, leaving Oliver to gather up the drawings and fight off the disappointed members of the crowd who had planned on viewing them at closer quarters, and leaving Congressman Brower and Joe Shelby to deal with unhappy reporters. Some people crowded onto the steps and pushed their way into the mayor's office. Two reporters pushed their way to Brower, and Shelby, going against the flow, made his way to the bottom of the stairs.

As he stepped clear of the crowd, thinking that he had made good his escape, he found his path blocked by two men. American Indians by their looks, he thought. One was an old man, Shelby guessed about eighty. The other was probably in his late twenties, maybe thirty or so.

"Hello," said Shelby. "Excuse me."

"Mr. Shelby," said the young man.

"Yeah?"

"Mr. Shelby, we came to see you."

"Oh? What about?"

"My grandfather here, he wants to tell you something."

"What is it?" Shelby asked.

The old man drew himself up and looked Shelby straight in the eyes.

"What you're getting ready to do," he said, "is very dangerous."

"No," Shelby said. "It's a pretty big job, but there's not anything especially dangerous about it. We know what we're doing."

"He doesn't mean that," said the young man. "He's not talking about the kind of work you do."

"Well, what, then?" Shelby asked. "What are you talking about?"

"It's a dangerous spot down there," said the old man.

"A dangerous spot? Yeah. Well, it won't be when we get it cleaned up."

"The place is bad," said the old man.

"Wait a minute," said Shelby. "Are you trying to tell me that we're planning to go to work on some sacred site or something like that? Because if that's what it is, you should have brought this up at the public hearings. That's what they're for. It's too late to stop this project now. Is that what it is? Are we messing around with holy land or something?"

"Not holy," said the old man. "Bad."

"We didn't know about the public hearings," said the young man. "We didn't know anything about this until today. We just came to town to buy some stuff and seen all the people down at the beach, so we went down to see what was happening. First we knew of it."

"Okay," said Shelby, "but what do you mean that it's a bad place? What kind of bad place? What could happen?"

"I don't know," said the old man, "but you should leave it alone."

"Look," said Shelby, "I know how most Indians feel about the Corps. I don't blame you. I know that the Corps has a pretty damn bad record when it comes to dealing with Indians. I think that's changing. I hope it is. I respect you and your beliefs, and if you can give me something a little more substantial to go on, maybe we can hold off on this deal and get it resolved. But I can't stop a major project just because you tell me that's a bad place. Do you understand?"

"That's all I know," said the old man. Then he turned to his grandson. "Let's go home," he said.

Chapter Two

Joe Shelby stood and stared after the two Indians as they walked away from him. They had left him with a sudden uneasy feeling. Why the hell couldn't he get a job without any kooky problems attached to it? The last one had bothered a bunch of environmentalists who had protested against the project, saying that it would upset the area's ecology. It wouldn't have been so bad had not Shelby felt deep inside himself, in spite of the environmental-impact study's findings to the contrary, that there was at least a fair chance that they were right.

The job before that one had involved a battle between private and public land interests, and Shelby suspected that the private interests would win out in the long run, even though the Corps wasn't supposed to work for private interests.

And now what? An Indian protest? An uprising? *Damn it*. He was a damn good engineer, and all he wanted was to just be let alone to do his job. He felt a hand touch his arm, and he jumped. Turning his head, he saw Kay standing there.

"What's wrong, Joe?" she asked.

"Oh, nothing," he said, and he shrugged off an uncomfortable chill. He reached out to put an arm around his wife's shoulders. "Nothing, Kay," he said. "I'm all right. Look. Look there. You see those two Indians walking off down there? You see them?"

"Yes," she said.

"One old man and a younger one?" he asked. "Right there."

"Yes," she said, "and I saw you talking to them. What is it, Joe?"

"The old man," said Shelby, "he told me not to work here."

"What?" she asked. "What for?"

"He told me not to do this job," said Shelby. "Said that beach down there—said it was a bad place. That's all."

"Well, what in the world did he mean by that?" Kay asked.

"Hell, I don't know," said Shelby. "I don't think he did either. I asked him. He said that's all he knows. It's a bad place. That's all."

"Well," said Kay, "I don't think you should let it bother you, if that's all he could say."

"No. No, I guess not," Shelby said. He was still staring after the Indians, even though they had turned a corner and were no longer in sight.

Kay tugged at his arm. "Come on," she said. "Let's go."

They strolled along the street in the direction of the hotel at which they were registered.

"I just can't help thinking about those damn birds," said Shelby. "Those damn crows back down there at the beach."

"They were acting pretty peculiar, weren't they?" said Kay.

"It doesn't make any sense," Shelby said. "They weren't guarding a nest or anything like that. Just sitting on that damned old pole and carrying on that way. What do you make of it?"

"Now, don't go trying to make sense out of the way crows act," Kay warned.

"No. I won't," he said. "You're right. Let's just forget it."

*   *   *

It was early evening, and Joe Shelby picked his careful way down the path from the top of the cliff to the beach. Everything was still. Unreal. More like a painted drop for the theater than a real stretch of beach looking out onto the ocean. The two crows sat immobile on top of the pole. Silent sentries. Shelby had the eerie sensation that they were watching him. The silence was oppressive, and Shelby thought that there was something unnatural and just a bit spooky about it.

He wasn't all that far from the noises of the city above. He should have been able to hear at least some of it. Staring at the crows on the pole, he began walking slowly through the sand. He kicked a half-buried gin bottle by accident, stumbled a little, and moved on. One crow puffed out its feathers as Shelby reached a point halfway between where he had started at the lower end of the path and the scummy water-line before the pole.

Ka.

One of the dark pair sounded a solemn and croaky warning. Shelby felt his skin crawl, but he kept walking until he reached the wire-rope reel, then stood beside it looking directly at the frowsy crows on the end of the weathered pole. They began to fidget and alternately flapped their wings.

Big suckers, he thought.

Ka. Ka.

"What the hell's bothering you?" he shouted. "God damn crows."

Ka.

"Get out of here."

Ka. Ka.

Shelby looked around his feet at the litter on the beach. He found a walnut-size, smooth rock and picked it up. He hefted it for size and weight. He looked back at the birds.

"Go on," he shouted.

Ka.

He took aim and threw the rock, missing pole and crows. It splashed into the water a few feet beyond and to the right of the pole. One crow hopped on the pole. The other ruffled its feathers.

Ka. Ka.

Shelby picked up another rock and aimed. He pitched it hard, and it bounced with a thud off the pole about a foot from the top. Both crows flew off the pole and shouted hysterically at him, then perched once again on the ancient wood.

What are those bastards up to? Shelby asked himself.

He gathered several missiles, lining them up on top of the reel—a couple more rocks, a beer bottle, a large rusty bolt—and he threw them one after the other, striking the pole twice, shouting all the while.

"Go on. Get. Get the hell out of here."

Ka. Ka. Ka.

The crows were in a panic. One of them flew up high and made a long dive for Shelby's head, coming so close that he swung wildly at it with his fist.

"God damn," he said. "Son of a bitch!"

Ka.

He watched as the crow circled above. He braced himself for another assault, but it never came. Shelby sat down heavily on the dirty reel, panting from all his sudden exertion. The crows settled down to resume their vigil on top of the pole.

The something up there was bothering the crows again. He could tell. He hoped that it would bother them to death, whatever it was. He could hear them squawking and hollering up there, and although the water was murky and the sky above was gray, he could just make out their hateful shapes flapping about above him. He could hear their frantic *ka ka*s. He hated them, and he liked whatever it was that had gotten them so agitated. Then something struck the pole, and he felt the vibrations in his own guts and in his groin. A sharp, tingling sensation.

"Ahh," he gasped in surprise, and he saw the bubbles rise from his voice.

Ding.

It struck again, this time harder, and the tingling was sharper. The wretched crows were screaming and fluttering around.

Ding.

He thought then that his entire insides were vibrating. He could feel the irritating vibrations working their way clear down to his toenails and all the way back up to his teeth. He was getting angry. He sucked in a deep breath, swallowing vile-tasting salt water, and then he began to thrash about wildly there on the ocean floor with all his might.

Then Shelby saw the pole begin to tremble, and the frantic crows began again to flap and hop and scold. He stood, staring at the strange phenomena in astonished disbelief, and he thought about the old Indian man he had met in front of the Mayor's office.

"It's a bad place," he had said.

"It could have been just a small tremor," said Kay. "You know, an earthquake."

"That would make sense just by itself, babe,"

said Shelby, "but it's a hell of a lot of weird co-incidence, don't you think?"

"They're very common out here," she said.

"Weird coincidences?" he said.

"No, silly," she said. "I meant earthquakes. Especially the little tremors. This is southern California, you know."

"Yeah," he said. "I know. At least, I thought I knew, until all this weird shit started coming at me here all at once. Now I—hell, I just don't know."

He stretched himself out on the hotel bed with an audible sigh. Hotel beds never felt quite right to Shelby. Kay sat down on the edge of the bed and placed a cool hand on his forehead. It felt good. It helped.

"Let's go downstairs," she said, "and have a couple of drinks and get some supper. Just you and me. What do you say?"

"Yeah," said Shelby. "That might help. It sure as hell can't hurt."

Shelby slept fitfully that night. His dreams were filled with pairs of ugly black birds who stood in his path shouting at him to go around, to get away, to leave them alone; with old Indians with the solemn look of age-old prophets who warned him away, who spoke of "bad places," who had deep, sad lines on their ancient brown faces that reminded him of a bitter and cruel history and filled him with a painful sense of guilt; and with violent shakings of the earth.

Once he woke up and sat up in bed. Kay was sound asleep. He looked down at her, and he sighed, and he smiled softly. He put a hand lightly on her forehead, careful not to disturb her calm sleep. He was glad that her sleep wasn't troubled. She was a lovely lady who deserved the best that he could give her in this life.

"Coincidence," she said, he thought. *Coincidence. Hell. It's too damn strange. The warnings. What is it about that place? Those damn birds? I've never seen birds act like that before. Never. Then add to that the old man's warning and—*

What the hell? Kay's probably right. Just coincidence. What else could it be? Like she said, who the hell can explain crow behavior anyway? And I sure as hell can't go to the boss and say two old crows and one old Indian told me to just forget about this job. I can't do that.

What would that look like on the damn report, anyway? Two and a half million smackers. Want to go out looking for a new job, Joe boy? Huh? Do you? No telling how damn long old phony Brower worked to push through the appropriations, and then there's all the people in this community. What they're looking forward to. And

*then the press. Oh, my God, the press. They'd
have themselves a real field day, now wouldn't
they? Forget it. Just forget it. Hell, boy, get some
sleep. Sleep. Sleep.*

Chapter Three

It was Monday morning, but, of course, he could not know that. He didn't know the year, or even the century. He didn't know how long he had been alive, or how long he had lain in the salty water. He lay there in a trance. Centuries had passed for him that way.

The behavior of the crows and the other recent noises from above had given him a slight respite, a bit of hope and anxiety, the thought that maybe something big was about to happen, but it had not lasted. The old boredom had set back in quickly. The numbness had returned.

And the trance had at last overcome him. The welcome, soothing, blessed trance.

Just before he had slipped into the trance, he had thought that his worst enemy was hope. The crows and the noises had given him hope, the first he had experienced in centuries, but it had turned out to be a false hope, a vague and unreal dream, and he was devastated. He had wanted no more of hope.

He had longed for the sense of nothingness that came with trance. He had wanted to slip back into one that would last until the end of the world. And then it had come, and now he was adrift in an endless ocean of unknowing, unseeing, unfeeling oblivion.

And then the crows began to scream again. At first their irascible shrieks had seemed far away and faint, but they drove themselves relentlessly into his consciousness. They battered his brain. They echoed and re-echoed, resounded and reverberated until they had utterly destroyed his blessed state.

And now he was no longer comfortably adrift. He was once again firmly anchored to the bottom of the ocean by the hated pole, and he was fully conscious and wide awake and alert, and he hated it. The awful, rasping *ka ka*s seemed to be right inside his head, bouncing from one side of his skull to the other as if it were a hollow, empty vessel and they were rubber balls.

BRASS

He shouted, and the noise he made was drowned in the water that was all the world he knew, and the bubbles he produced drifted upward, taunting him with his own impotence. He wondered if his shout was captured in the bubbles, and if, when the bubbles reached the top of the water, they would then burst and release his raging voice to the outside world.

If only he could catch the crows. If only he could hold them in his hands. One in each hand. Feeling their little hearts pounding inside their downy chests. He would squeeze. He would make them *ka ka* just once more. He would. One last time. Perhaps he would not squeeze them to death, though. No. Perhaps instead he would bite off their heads.

No. He would bite off only one head, allowing the other captive crow to watch in horror-stricken anticipation as he chewed the head, crunching the small skull, eyes, beak, brains, and all. Then he would pluck the second one naked of all its feathers, break its legs and its useless wings, and set it back upon its perch. He laughed at the scene he had imagined for himself, and the laugh was drowned, and the bubbles rose, and the *ka*s kept bouncing in his tormented brain.

And then there was a noise. It was a new noise. It was similar to other noises he had heard from time to time. He had not heard them at first, centuries ago when he had first been captured and pinned down. They were not noises he had known in the long-ago, primitive and real world, when he had walked carefree and easy on the face of the earth, and he had not heard them until long after the strange, new life-forms began to swim above his head. As he measured time in his mind, he had only begun to hear them recently, yesterday perhaps. Strange and harsh noises he could not identify.

And they were not all alike, not exactly. There were subtleties, shades of difference. Perhaps they were the sounds of some new and massive beasts that roamed the earth. Sometimes they sounded far, far off. Occasionally near. Once, one such noise had visited him in the company of a large shadow that floated on the surface just above. That had been the loudest of them all.

But now he heard a whole array of these same kinds of sounds, and in his wounded breast his heart began to pulse with renewed and anxious vigor. He felt it pound, and its beating began to rival the bouncing *ka*s still thumping in his brain. The anticipation had returned. The anxiety was intense. Something had to happen. Something. Something soon. Something. Anything.

* * *

"All right, Bud," said Shelby, "get that damned equipment down there and have them just scrape all that shit into one big pile. While you've got that going on, get somebody to cutting us a road down from the shelf over here. We'll need that to get the trucks down here in order to haul the junk off."

"I think you and me can go on out into the bay and study our problem out there while they're doing all that," said Bud. "If you want to."

"Yeah. Okay," said Shelby. "Let's do that. You get them started up here, and then you and me will take the boat out and look it over."

While Bud trotted up the path to the top of the cliff to begin shouting orders at the crew waiting with the big machines, Shelby casually surveyed the mess he was about to tackle. He heard two or three big engines up above kick over and rev, and then he heard the crows. He looked out at the pole, and there they sat, looking back at him, screaming their warnings.

One opened its wings menacingly. The little 'dozer with the front-end scoop lurched over the edge of the shelf onto the footpath and roared its way down onto the beach. The rest would have to wait for the graders to widen the path into a road for larger vehicles.

As the 'dozer bounced and jockeyed itself into position to begin scooping and shoving its way through the astonishing array of cast-off testimonials to the wealth and waste of the twentieth century, the crows increased their volume. Up above, the graders were already lashing at the edge of the shelf.

"Joe," said Bud.

Shelby turned abruptly.

"What?" he snapped.

He thought at once that he had spoken too quickly, too sharply. He hoped that Bud hadn't noticed, that the roaring engines had covered his nervous tone.

"The boys got the boat down on the beach here for us," Bud said. "You ready to go out?"

"Yeah," Shelby said. "Let's go."

Shelby followed Bud along the water's edge to a spot of nasty beach where the boat waited, its bow just in the water, nudging scum. Shelby stepped in and moved to the bow seat.

"You can drive, buddy," he said.

"Okay," said Bud. He waved at two men back up on the beach. "Shove us out," he said. He stepped into the boat and sat back by the engine. The two men he had hailed trotted down and pushed the boat out onto the water.

Bud nodded his thanks, picked up an oar, and pushed against the soft, sandy bottom to move the fourteen-foot Starcraft out into deeper water. Then he replaced the oar, now dripping scum, lowered the big Evinrude engine, and pulled the starter rope.

On the third pull, the motor roared to life. Bud revved it a few times, then headed the boat for even deeper waters, and the ever-watchful crows shrieked out their stern disapproval. As Bud swung the Starcraft around to head out toward the reef, he made a pass too near the pole for the comfort of the birds. One swooped down toward the brash offenders.

"Hey," Shelby shouted, slapping wildly with both arms. He had to duck his head to keep the angry crow from flying right in his face. It rose up, circled, and tried again.

Ka. Ka.

On the second try it passed close by Shelby's ear. He felt the wind from its flight, heard a loud *ka* resound, and lashed out at it with both hands. He felt foolish. He was being made a fool of in front of his whole work crew by a crow.

"Goddamn it," he shouted. "Get the hell away from here, Bud."

Bud goosed the Evinrude and headed out toward the reef. The scruffy black birds, apparently satisfied for the time being that the boat and its unwelcome occupants had gotten far enough away from them, reperched themselves on the pole.

Ka, ka, they called in triumph.

"Bud," shouted Shelby, "shut this thing off."

Bud cut the engine, and the boat rocked mildly on the dirty water of the inlet.

"Forget the goddamned reef for now," said Shelby. "Do you think this thing's got the power to pull up that damn pole?"

"We could try it," said Bud. "If it ain't, we can always run a line back to the beach and pull it with the 'dozer."

"Let's go back in," said Shelby, "but swing wide of that damn pole."

Back on the beach, Shelby climbed the hill to his pickup for the .22 Magnum Ruger revolver he kept in the glove box, while Bud gathered up the other equipment they would need. Soon they were back in the water, this time wearing hard hats, and they headed straight for the pole. Shelby fired the revolver, the bullet striking the pole just under where one crow sat. Splinters flew from the pole, and the crow, with an eerie, humanlike scream, jumped straight up into the air.

Ka, ka, ka, the crows both screamed.

Shelby fired again. The crows flew high. Then one made a sudden dive for Shelby's head. He ducked, and he felt a solid thunk against the plastic hat from the impact as the crow hit, then flew on. He looked up and fired again, a wild shot for which he was ashamed. He knew he couldn't hit a crow in flight from a rocking boat with the revolver.

Bud pulled the Starcraft up close beside the pole, now abandoned by the frenzied crows, who circled overhead and cursed the scene below.

Ka, ka.

He slapped a heavy canvas strap around the pole and hooked it to the end of a chain. The chain was attached to the stern of the Starcraft.

"Hit it," said Shelby.

Ka, ka.

Bud eased the boat away from the pole until the chain was taut, then nudged the engine a bit more.

The almost deafening roar was right above him now, and now the foolish crows were wild, and the water wafted back and forth and made his body sway with its undulating motions. He saw it, whatever it was, like a great shadow on the surface of the slime in which he lay. It was like the other he had seen before. A large shape moving overhead accompanied by a roar. Some new sea animal swimming on the top and growling?

He heard a loud, sharp crack, and something smacked against his pole. He felt the pang. The vibrations raced throughout his body. Then he heard a second and a third. He thought that someone up above was breaking trees. He shuddered with excitement and a wild, desperate anticipation. Then he felt a tug. Yes. Something was happening.

The pole lurched, and the lurching wrenched his body. It lurched again. It hurt his guts. He groaned with the pain. It was like the original, the long-ago pain, the pain he had felt that awful day when they had pinned him down. Another lurch.

He screamed and shot forth frothy bubbles from his cavernous mouth. Then there was an even greater and more violent wrenching of the pole, and then the pulling was steady and sustained. He thought that he'd be cut in half, and suddenly he was moved. The pole was ripped out of its moorings. Great clouds of sand and gravel and debris exploded all around him. He couldn't see. The clouds were too thick, and the pain caused blackness all around. He couldn't tell up from down.

The hated pole that had been almost a part of him for so long was then ripped on through, and he was suddenly and unexpectedly free at last, but he was tumbling in the dark, confusing waters, and the agony in his tormented guts reached levels he had never known before. His hands went automatically to the open wound—

the large hole that went all the way through his body. He felt his raw and bleeding flesh and his ragged innards, and he roared out in pain and rage.

Chapter Four

He was furious, in dreadful pain, frightened
and confused, and he automatically reverted to
his ancient protective instinct. Tumbling wildly
head-over-heels in the murky water in a bewil-
dered rage, he began to protect himself in the
only way he knew against the unknown dangers
that might await him.

His arms and legs began to cramp and draw
up. His skin, already tough and thick, hardened
and grew mottled with gnarled lumps. His teeth
became sharpened and elongated as his jaws
extended to form a long and grotesque snout.

From the lower end of his spine, a great and powerful tail grew, and it began to lash about and further roil the already troubled, filthy waters.

"What the hell's going on down there?" said Shelby.

Bud had cut the engine to an idle, having dragged the long pole out of its moorings. The crows circled high above in seeming confusion, their *ka*s having assumed a forlorn, despairing tone. But the spot where the pole had stood was now a bubbling eddy, its violence sustained much too long to be explained by the relatively minor disruption caused by the pulling up of the pole.

"Get to shore," Shelby shouted. "Come on. Hit it, Bud."

And then the great beast rose up out of the water as if shot from a cannon somewhere below the surface, exposing almost his entire body to their astonished view. He seemed suspended in the air for a chilling moment. Bud sat transfixed, his reflexes dulled by the incredible sight before his eyes.

The huge beast descended with a great belly flop, sending up a surge of waves that rocked the boat wildly. Bud then snapped out of his momentary trance. His stunned brain at last sent a signal to his hand. *Get out*, it said. But it was too late. Before his trembling hand could respond, the great tail of the beast swung around and slapped him from the boat.

Bud screamed, and Shelby shouted and made a dive for the stern. Desperately, he grabbed and turned the throttle, sending the Starcraft in a crazy circle before he could straighten himself up and set his course for shore. The beast, seeming to skim the top of the water, amazingly agile for its bulk, lunged at Bud, its great jaws opened wide, and snapped them shut around his flailing, broken torso. A dark red stain seeped out and tinged the murky water as Bud's screams ceased.

Shelby ran the boat aground and vaulted out onto the beach. The engine ground itself to an agonizing halt, its propeller raking gritty sand. Two of the crew ran up to stand beside Shelby. Others were standing on the rise or running down the footpath.

"Oh, Jesus," said Shelby.

"What the hell is that?" said one man.

"An alligator," said the other. "A goddamned monster alligator."

"In the ocean?"

"It's out there, ain't it?"

"Jesus," said Shelby.

"I never seen one that big."

Out in the water, the giant gator chomped and lashed, finishing off his grisly meal.

Shelby's horror suddenly turned to rage. He remembered the Ruger in the boat, turned, and ran for it. He grabbed it up, but just as he turned to fire, the beast rose up again and bashed itself back down into the water, sinking out of sight. There was nothing left to shoot at.

"Go on, Chuck," shouted Shelby. "Get the hell up to town. Get the cops. Do something."

He held the revolver ready, looking out frantically over the now sinister inlet, as Chuck ran toward the footpath. The crows had vanished from the sky. They were gone. The rest of the stunned work crew had gathered along the beach at the edge of the water, their unbelieving stares searching for further evidence of the unreal horror they had just witnessed.

Down below the murk, the great beast nuzzled itself lethargically into the ooze at the bottom of the bay. He swallowed down one last chunk of the man flesh, and he felt good. He had only begun to make up for all those centuries, all that seemingly endless wait, the suffering, the anguish, the dreadful loneliness. He would wait yet awhile. There were still more people out there on the beach. They were not like any people he had ever seen before, but he was not surprised at that. Had he not watched life-forms change beneath the sea? And they had those strange, new, large animals that growled so

fiercely. He had waited an eternity down there.
He could wait a little longer.

Shelby was still stalking the beach, gun in hand,
when he heard the sirens whining up above on
the shelf. He didn't look back to see them. His
wild eyes kept searching the water for some
sign of the monstrous gator that had eaten Bud.
Harvey Chase, the local chief of police, slightly
overweight, trudged down the path and wad-
dled out through the sand to come up and stand
beside Shelby.

"Shelby," he said.

Shelby didn't turn to face him. He kept scan-
ning the waters. Something about the expression on his face and the tension in his frame
worried Chase.

"Shelby," he said. "I need to talk to you."

"Yeah," said Shelby. "Go ahead."

"I've got some men here, Shelby," said Chase.
"They'll take over now."

"Huh?"

"Put down the gun and talk to me," said
Chase, raising his voice.

Chase took hold of the Ruger, and Shelby
looked at him for the first time. He slowly relaxed his grip, allowing the chief to take the
weapon.

"Now," said Chase, "tell me what happened
here."

"Hell," said Shelby, "you won't believe it. I saw it. I saw it, and I don't believe it."

"The man you sent to get me," said the Chief, "said something about a giant gator."

"That's what it was, Chief," Shelby said. "That's just what it was. A giant alligator. Biggest damn thing I ever saw."

"You lost a man?"

Shelby nodded.

"Bud," he said. "It just ate him. That thing. That damn thing. It ate him, right there in front of all of us. I—I don't know what was wrong with me. I could have gotten the gun sooner and shot it, if only I'd been thinking straight. You know? I had the gun in the boat. I—I just don't know. I could have saved him."

"You don't know that for sure," said Chase. "Try to calm down now. Take it easy. You said you had the gun with you in the boat?"

"Yeah," Shelby said. "Well, we went out in the water to pull up that pole. Well, no, I mean, we didn't go out there in the first place to pull up the pole, we went out there to check out that reef, but the damn crows attacked us, so—"

"Hold on, there," said Chase. "You were attacked by crows?"

"Yeah," said Shelby. "The crows on the pole."

"Hold on," the chief said. He walked over to another cop standing on the beach. "Phil," he said, "I want you to take over here. Put some of the boys to looking over the area, see what they can see, and get statements from everyone here about what happened. Right now I'm taking Shelby back over to the office with me to talk about this thing. Okay?"

"Okay, Chief," Phil said.

"Oh, Phil," said Chase. "One more thing. When you get all that done, leave a couple of men down here to watch the area."

As Chase drove away from the shelf overlooking the blighted beach with Shelby in his patrol car, about twenty yards north of where Phil and the other policemen still searched in vain for evidence of any kind related to what had taken place there, a muskrat pushed his nose out of the water up onto the sandy shore. A thin, green film of scum stretched across his face and head as he crawled out of the bay and scurried to the nearby shell of a burned-out 1950 Mercury lying on its top.

He scampered inside the hard skin of the big, dead animal and watched intently the movements of the people on the beach. He recognized them as people, but they were not like any people he had ever seen before. Their clothing was strange to his eyes, and what showed of their skin was deathly pale.

He wondered what had become of the people he remembered, those who had walked the earth before, back in the old days, the ancient days. How long ago had it been? He didn't know. He realized that if he wanted to move again among humankind, he would be obliged to take upon himself this new and ugly form.

"Sit down, Shelby," said Chase as he moved to the chair behind his desk. "Now, just try to stay calm and tell me exactly what happened. Start at the beginning, and take your time."

Shelby sat and rubbed his face. Where was the beginning? It seemed so long ago. So damned long ago. Could it really have been only three days? Just three? He shook his head to try to clear his brain. It didn't work. *Start at the beginning," he said. Where is that? The crows? The crows.* How could he tell this cop about the crows? *But that's the beginning.*

"There was a pole out there in the water," he said. "Out in the bay. Sticking straight up out of the water. Well, the other day, when the mayor and the congressman made the announcement to the crowd down there on the beach—you were there, you remember—the damn crows were on the pole. Two of them. They were hollering around. You remember? Acting crazy."

Chase remembered, all right. He had, like everyone else there, noticed the peculiar behavior of the crows, but he failed to see the relevance of that to what had just happened down there at the beach. He didn't answer, and Shelby went on with his tale.

"There was an old Indian here in town," he said, "right after that, when we came up here. He had a young guy with him, Indian guy. Anyway, the old one, he told me not to work down there. 'It's a bad place,' he said. Bad place. He wouldn't say anything more. Just that it's a bad place."

Shelby stood up and paced across the floor, rubbing his forehead.

"This is crazy," he said. "It doesn't make any sense. I think I'm going nuts."

"You're doing all right," said Chase. "Keep going."

"I went back down there," Shelby said. "By myself. They were still there."

"The crows?" said Chase.

"Still sitting on that pole," said Shelby. "I threw some rocks at them. Tried to chase them off. They flew at me. Does that make sense? Crows guarding a pole? I guess that's what they were doing. Does that make any sense? This is crazy."

Chase took a pack of Marlboros out of his shirt pocket and held it out toward Shelby.

"You want a cigarette?" he asked.

Shelby did not smoke, but he walked over to the desk and extended his hand.

"Yeah. Thanks," he said.

Chase flipped his Bic and held it out for Shelby to get a light. Shelby drew in a lungful of smoke and exhaled it slowly, while Chase took out a cigarette for himself and lit it. Shelby went back over to the chair and sat down again.

"Go on," said Chase.

"When we went to work this morning," Shelby said, "they really started acting up."

"The crows?" Chase asked.

"Yeah," said Shelby. "The crows. Bud and I went out on the water to go check the reef, and they flew at me again. I got pissed off. I decided then to go ahead and pull the damn pole up, so we went back in to get some equipment—I got my gun—and we went out and pulled it up. I shot at them. The damn crows. Never hit one. Can't hit shit with that damned Ruger.

"When the pole came up, the water started . . . I don't know—it was like it was boiling in that one spot. I don't mean it was hot. Not that. But it was rolling, bubbling, you know? And then—"

Shelby stood again and walked to the window, where he stood with his back to the police chief.

"And then?" said Chase.

"That . . . thing came up," said Shelby, turning suddenly to face Chase, his eyes wild. "That giant alligator. It came right up out of the water there where it was boiling, bubbling, whatever.

Came up and lashed its tail around. Knocked Bud out of the boat.

"I had a gun. I should have used it. But I panicked, I guess. I don't know. I jumped for the engine controls and ran away. I raced to shore. And that thing—it . . . it ate him. It ate him. That's all. I got the gun, but it had gone back under. It didn't come back up."

Chase took a long drag off his cigarette, then rolled the ashes carefully off its end into the ashtray on his desk. He looked up at Shelby.

"You're right about one thing," he said.

"What do you mean, one thing?" Shelby asked.

"It's crazy," said Chase. "Doesn't make any sense. We can't write that up in a report. Can't release it to the press. Don't tell this story again, Shelby. Not to anyone. The part that we can tell is bad enough, and I wouldn't let it out if I could help it. One of your men was killed by an alligator. That's it. How an alligator got into the ocean here, we don't know. We'll look for it, and warn people away from this stretch of beach here until we find it. That's all. You got that?"

"Well, yeah, but I—"

"No buts, Shelby," said Chase. "That's it. Your work on the beach can go on, but stay out of the water—stay off the water until we get this thing cleared up. That reef work will just have to wait."

Shelby thought that it could all wait, the whole damned project—for a hell of a long time. He took a last drag on his cigarette, burning it down to the filter, as Chase glanced out through the window in his office door and saw Phil walk in.

"Excuse me," said Chase, and he walked out into the squad room, closing the office door behind himself. He talked to Phil for a few minutes, then returned to Shelby. He stood in front of his desk a moment, leaned back against it, and expelled a long and audible sigh.

"Shelby," he said at last, "if you are crazy, so is your whole damn crew. They all saw the same things you did. I just told my officer there to get back down to the beach and tell the rest of them the same thing I just told you. To keep their damn mouths shut. Now, is there anything else you can think of to tell me?"

"No," said Shelby. "Hell, I told you all of it. Wait. Wait a minute. It had a big, ugly scar. Yeah. On its belly. A big scar."

Chapter Five

He was inside the external skeleton of the big
bug that lay on its back on the beach—the one
into which he had crept earlier. It was getting
dark, and most of the pallid people were gone.
Only a few of them were left out on the beach,
the ones who dressed all in blue. One of these
men in blue wandered along the water's edge
until he had reached a spot on the opposite side
of the big animal's shell from that of all his companions. He looked back at his companions for
a second, then started to urinate in the sand.

The form skulking inside the skin was himself

again, back in his own near-human form, and he was naked. His horrible belly wound was now only a nasty scar. He couldn't see his own back, of course, but he had reached around to feel it. It, too, was scar red.

He got onto his hands and knees inside the shell that lay upon its back and crept out through the large opening in its side until he was right behind the lone man in blue, who was in the process of putting his tool away. He stood, his bare feet clutching at the wet, slimy sand, and he flung his great right arm around the man's neck and growled. The man started to scream, but the scream was quickly stifled. He cracked the man's neck with a slight jerk of his powerful arm, and the body sagged lifeless in his grasp. He heard someone back down the beach shouting.

"What was that?"

He had never heard the language before, and it sounded harsh and ugly to his ears, yet he understood it perfectly. He looked in the direction from which the voice had come, and he saw two men in blue running through the sand toward him. Each held a small, strange device in his hand.

"Up there," one shouted. "By the car."

"God," said the other. "What is it?"

The men pointed at him with the things in their hands, and then he heard loud, cracking

61

noises. They were like the ones he had heard before, when he had still been pinned down, but they were much louder, not being filtered through the nasty water before reaching his ears. Then something bit him on the arm and made him yell and drop the body. He turned to run, but he remembered why he had killed the man. He picked up the body and threw it lightly over his left shoulder. Then he ran.

Mayor Purchase stalked into the Police Department and headed straight for the office of the chief. The receptionist and the desk sergeant both made valiant efforts to stop him and speak with him, but he passed them by too quickly and too brusquely. He flung open Chase's office door and took two long strides across the room to the desk. He aimed his index finger at Chase's head.

"What the hell is going on around here?" he demanded.

"What do you mean, Mayor?" said Chase.

Shelby still sat in the chair against the wall, but Purchase seemed not to notice his presence in the room.

"Alligators eating people," Purchase said, "magic crows, the work stopped down at the beach. What's going on?"

"There was apparently an alligator in the

bay," said Chase. "One of Mr. Shelby's crew allegedly was killed."

"Allegedly?" said Purchase. "How is someone
allegedly killed? Is he killed or isn't he?"

"I've been told that he was killed," said Chase.
"There were witnesses. There is no body. It was
apparently eaten."

"Well, what are you doing about it?" the
Mayor asked.

"We're investigating, Mr. Mayor," said Chase.
"We're looking for the animal to kill it."

"Damn it, Chase," said the mayor, "we've got
lots of press people in town. We've got Congressman Brower. We got ourselves a major
project to get going here. You've got to stop
these rumors now."

"I've already instructed all the witnesses to
keep quiet," said Chase. "The only story we'll
release is that a man was killed by a stray alligator. We'll have to warn people away from the
beach until it's been found and killed."

"If you've told everyone to keep their yap
shut," said Purchase, "then how the hell did I
find out about it so soon? Huh? Tell me that."

Chase stood up and walked around his desk
to face the mayor.

"That's what I'd like to know," he said. "Who
told you?"

"Never you mind that," Purchase said. "Whoever it was, he did what he should have done.

I'm the mayor of this city. You should have told me right away."

Chase took out his pack of Marlboros and fired one up.

"Mr. Mayor," he said, blowing smoke, "I've only just now finished interviewing Mr. Shelby here. I'm trying to ascertain just exactly what's occurred. I haven't had time to go running for you. I'm doing my job the way it should be done, and if that's not good enough for you, well, then, you can look for another chief of police."

At the mention of Shelby's name, the mayor suddenly turned on him, probably to avoid the challenge thrown at him by the chief.

"What are you trying to pull?" he said.

Shelby came up out of his chair fast enough to cause Purchase to step back.

"Damn you," said Shelby. "Damn you and your beach. What do you mean, just what do you mean, what am I trying to pull? I just watched a man, a man I knew and worked with, I just watched him die. A horrible, ghastly death. What the hell do you mean by suggesting that I'm up to something? God damn you all the way to hell."

Chase stepped in between Shelby and the mayor. He was afraid that Shelby might punch the mayor in the nose, and he wouldn't have blamed him a bit if he did. Still, he couldn't allow it to happen right there in his office.

"Mr. Shelby," he said, "it's all right. Everyone's upset here right now. Why don't you go on back to your hotel room now and try to relax? I'll let you know if I need you. Go on, now."

Shelby turned and left the office, and Chase shoved the extra chair toward Purchase.

"Sit down, please, Mr. Mayor," he said, "and let's talk this over."

On the shelf overlooking the beach, the naked thing that looked like a man with the frightful scar on his front and back scaled the chain-link fence and ran inside one of the empty houses. He tossed the body he still carried with him onto the floor and looked outside. The other men in blue were trying to climb the fence.

Patrolman Brown was just putting a foot on top of the fence, ready to swing on over, and Sutherland was only halfway up, when a giant hawklike bird swooped down, seemingly out of nowhere. Brown felt a massive talon grip his head. Its grip was like that of a vise, but it had claws.

Brown screamed and flailed at the monster and lost his balance, but he didn't fall. Instead he was lifted into the air as the massive winged beast soared upward. The claws pierced Brown's skin, and blood ran freely down all sides of his head. For a moment all he could see was sky and the feathers of the thing that bore him fluttering overhead. Then everything went black.

There was a loud pop, and the fragile skull was squashed, exploding blood and brains. Down below, Sutherland huddled on the ground against the fence and, covering his head, braved an upward glance. He saw the headless body plummet. He saw no bird.

He walked into their town, and it was not like any town that he had ever seen. The surface of the earth was hard and hot in places, covered with a substance he did not know. The great bugs ran growling up and down the streets, and people sat inside them. The houses were large and built of unfamiliar materials, and all the people that he saw at first were sickly pale like those he'd seen down at the beach, but soon he saw some others. Some were black, and some looked more or less like the people he had known before, except that they wore the same peculiar clothing as did all the others.

But he was like them now. He, too, was pale and sickly ugly like most of those around. And he had clothes like theirs, a blue suit and a hat. He also had the terribly uncomfortable shoes, and the thing they pointed was hanging in a case upon his hip. And he could talk like they did. He had tried. He had been pleased to discover that his special talent, his gift, had not been lost during that eternity in the sea.

He walked into the town, bold and full of curiosity, and he did not feel at all conspicuous. He felt safe in his disguise. He had worried at first that these people would spot him as a stranger and ask him questions. That would have happened in the days long gone that he remembered on the earth, but once again he discovered that these were not like any people he had known.

They hurried past one another without speaking, without even seeming to notice each other. He wondered for a moment if they could even see, but they didn't run into each other, or the houses, or get in front of the massive bugs that carried some of them around.

He was safe then, and he was glad to be once again among the human kind—even such seemingly inexplicable ones. He would learn their habits. A woman walked toward him on the walkway, an old one with gray hair and no color to her skin. She smiled as she approached and looked straight at his face.

"Hello," she said.

"Hello," he responded.

So, he thought, *they do speak greetings sometimes, and I answered. I can talk their talk, and everything's all right. My disguise is perfect.* Then he heard a shout just at his back.

"Hey, watch out, man!"

He looked over his shoulder just in time to dodge a young man who seemed to glide along the surface of the earth. He was one of the pallid ones and had long, yellow, flowing hair. His feet stood still on a long, flat thing with wheels, and he carried in one hand a big, black box from which came awful, screaming sounds accompanied by other strange, chaotic noises, and he wondered once again at the changes the world had suffered during his long, enforced absence. He felt a kinship with the earth. He pitied her.

He noticed that some of the people went around nearly naked, especially the younger ones, both male and female, and that would have seemed to him more natural had it not been for the wretched, washed-out hue of their skin. Just then two men approached him, wearing blue suits just like the one he wore. He smiled, just as the old, fish-belly-colored woman had smiled at him.

"Hello," he said.

One man moved to his right side, the other to his left. They poised themselves for danger and pointed those peculiar little black things at him, like the ones he had seen at the beach, like the one he now carried at his side. He thought that maybe they were the things that made the cracking sound, and that one of them had somehow bit him in the arm, but he couldn't be sure about that.

"Put your hands up," said one.

"Why?" he said, and he smiled.

"Get them up," the man said.

He shrugged and lifted his hands.

"Higher," said the man.

Why not? he thought. *Perhaps it's a new game, or one of their strange customs*. But the two men appeared to be angry with him, and then another thought crossed his mind. If he did not obey, and if those things were the things that caused the bite, they might bite him again. He raised his hands higher.

"Get his gun, Frank," said the man. The other, Frank, who had not spoken all this time, took the heavy thing from its holder at his side. *Gun, he called it. Gun.*

"Come on," said the man called Frank.

"Where are we going?" he asked them.

"We're taking you to the station, bub," said the other.

He didn't know what kind of a place that station might be. He had much to learn, he realized, about this strange, new world. Well, he would go with them and see what he would see. He would learn some things. He walked along the crowded street, going where the two men guided him, and he noticed that the others, the people they passed and who passed them by, even those inside the giant bugs, were staring at them. Soon they came to a large house, and they went inside.

In his room at the hotel, Shelby paced the floor. Kay had never seen him so distraught, and she was worried about him. The business about Bud was horrible, of course, but she wished that she could find a way to calm her husband down.

"Maybe we should find a doctor," she said, "and get you a sedative or something."

"No," said Shelby. "I don't need anything. Not anything like that. I just—I feel like I ought to be doing something."

"Joe," she said, "what could you do?"

"I don't know," he said. "That's just the problem. I don't know."

"Let the police handle it, Joe," Kay said. "That's what they're trained for, and that's what they're paid to do. You're an engineer."

"But I saw it, Kay," Shelby said. "I saw it happen. It was Bud, and I was right there, and I had the warnings. I can't just sit here in this room and wait. I can't do that."

"You're going to make yourself crazy," she said.

"Hey," he said. "That's it."

"What?" she said. "Make yourself crazy?"

"No," he said. "No, hell. The warnings. Come on."

BRASS

Shelby grabbed his wife by the arm and pulled her to her feet, headed for the door.

"What?" she said. "Where are we going?"

"We're going to find that old Indian," said Shelby. "Come on."

Chapter Six

At the desk in the hotel lobby, Shelby got directions to the nearest Indian reservation—a rancheria, they called it. He and Kay got into the Dodge pickup and drove right out. Shelby had been on Indian reservations before in other parts of the country, so he wasn't surprised at what he found out there. He saw run-down housing, loose dogs, and, where the highway became the main street of a small reservation town, a block-long mini–skid row. Side roads were unpaved in the little town, which was really not quite on the rancheria, but rather, just at its edge.

Shelby parked the Dodge, got out, and stretched. He looked around. The Indians on the street looked at him, he thought, with distrust and suspicion. He never knew, on a reservation, whether those looks were real or were in his own mind. Whatever. He had expected the looks.

The Army Corps of Engineers had almost always encountered hostility on Indian reservations. Lately Shelby had begun to think that possibly it was deserved. He felt self-conscious and uncomfortable, but he had something to do. Something urgent.

He stepped up onto the sidewalk where a small grocery store and a bar stood side by side. Three drunks lounged beside the door to the bar. Shelby went inside the store and walked up to the counter, where he waited for the clerk to finish bagging groceries for his customer, a middle-aged Indian woman, and make her change.

"Hi," Shelby said as the woman turned to leave the store.

"Hello," said the clerk. "What can I do for you?"

"Well," said Shelby, "actually, I'm looking for someone."

"Got a name?" the clerk asked.

"No," said Shelby. "I mean, I don't know it. An old man and a young man, both Indians, were in the city three days ago. Last I saw of them, they were walking out of town. Back in this direction. I didn't see any vehicle."

"This is a small rancheria here," said the clerk, a white man, "but even so, that ain't much to go on."

"The old man," said Shelby, "he told me that the beach down there is a bad place. I'd like to find him and talk to him about it."

"You a college man?" asked the clerk. "Anthropologist or something?"

"No, I'm an engineer," said Shelby. "I'm, uh, I'm in charge of the project down there to construct a recreational beach."

"Oh, yeah," said the clerk. "I read about that. You ain't worrying about what that old man said, are you? Hell, I wouldn't pay no mind to what these old Indi'ns say. They got all kinds of superstitions. He might not even believe it himself. Might be just trying to get your goat. You know, they don't like you guys very much. The Corps of Engineers, I mean."

"Yeah," said Shelby, "I know. I'd still like to find this fellow and talk to him."

"Sorry," the clerk said. "I don't know who it might be."

"Yeah," said Shelby. "Well, thanks."

He stepped back out onto the sidewalk and looked up and down the street. *Damn*, he thought, *where do I go from here?* Kay leaned out the window on the passenger side of the pickup.

"Joe," she called.

Shelby walked over to her.

"What is it?" he said.

"I saw him," she said. "The young one. He just went around the corner down there."

Shelby ran around to the driver's side of the Dodge, jumped in, and started the car. He backed quickly out of the parking space, hit the brakes, jammed the gearshift lever into low, and squealed the tires. Rounding the corner, they saw the young man.

"There," said Kay.

Shelby slowed the Dodge and eased it up alongside the man.

"Hey," he said. "Hello there. You remember me?"

The Indian looked at Shelby.

"Oh, yeah," he said. "You're the guy with the Corps. What brings you out to the rez?"

"I need to talk to your grandfather," Shelby said.

Mayor Purchase stood up and turned his back on Chase. He assumed a posture of deep thought and held the pose for a moment.

"All right, Chief," he said. "I was a bit hasty, and I apologize for that, but you know how important this project is to me—to all of us. I'll get on out of here now and leave you to do your job, but I do want you to keep me informed. Agreed?"

"Of course, Mr. Mayor," Chase said.

Through his window Chase noticed three men enter the squad room. All were wearing blue uniforms, but one had his hands up in the air and another was holding his Police Special in his hand. Then Chase realized that he didn't recognize the man with his hands up.

"Shit," he said. "What now?"

"What is it?" said the mayor nervously.

The mayor ran to the door and looked out at the three men. Chase came up beside him and opened the door.

"Apple," he shouted. "Thomas. Get in here. Bring him with you."

The three men came into the office, and Chase closed the door behind them.

"Now, what the hell is this all about?" he demanded.

"We found this character out on Main Street, Chief," said the officer called Apple. "I never seen him before, and neither has Frank, but he's wearing one of our uniforms."

"Do you know him, sir?" asked Frank Thomas.

"Can't say that I do," said Chase. He walked up to the suspect. "That's Brown's badge. How the hell did you get that uniform and badge? Where's Officer Brown?"

The suspect didn't answer.

"Who are you?" Chase asked.

Still no answer.

"Well, put the cuffs on him and put your damn gun away," said Chase. "That's no way to bring in a damn suspect anyhow. Hell, you know that. Take him on out of here and book him. We'll get to the bottom of this."

While Apple still held his revolver on the suspect, Thomas took his handcuffs off his belt. He pulled the suspect's left arm down and around behind his back. Then he reached for the right arm.

The young Indian man, who had identified himself as Charlie Ramos, jumped into the back of the pickup and gave Shelby directions that led him out of town a few miles along an unpaved road.

"It's desolate out here," Kay said.

"Yeah," said Shelby. "We're getting out into the desert here," and he felt a twinge of guilt.

In the back of the pickup, Charlie Ramos leaned out over the edge and forward to shout at Shelby.

"Right up there," he said.

77

"Okay," Shelby yelled.

He pulled off the road to park in front of a small house. He guessed its size as twelve by twelve, and no more than eight feet high. In style it reminded him of the much larger, traditional houses of the tribes of the Northwest Coast. Constructed of vertically arranged, wide, rough planks, which Shelby thought to be hand hewn, it had a peaked roof, also made of planks, which extended far beyond the walls to form deep eaves and were held down on top by a variety of large, seemingly randomly placed stones. In place of a front door, a circular hole, just large enough for a man to crawl through, was cut in the front wall of the house, the lowest point of its circumference eighteen inches or so off the ground. Intricate designs were cut into the wood around the hole, their detail faded much from years of weathering.

Shelby opened the pickup door and got out, his footsteps causing little puffs of dust to rise up from the dry ground. Kay got out on the other side. A mongrel dog came running from behind the house and barked.

"Wait here," said Ramos, and he jumped out of the cargo box and walked up to the house. Bending over, he poked his head into the hole. "Grandpa," he said.

Shelby looked around the house as Ramos disappeared through the hole. Off to one side were the remains of a long-dead 1947 Nash. A variety of buckets, bottles, cans, and other discarded debris were scattered about in casual disarray. Something nagged at Shelby's conscience, and he put an arm around the shoulders of his wife and held her tightly to his side. Then he saw the old man's head reveal itself at the entry hole to look outside.

He had never before, of course, seen handcuffs, but with his arms suddenly wrenched around behind his back, he quickly surmised their purpose. The thought of being bound again so soon after his release sent a wave of panic and terror through his body that quickly settled in his loins. He flung his arms to the sides, slapping the gun from Apple's hand with his right and smashing Thomas's nose with his left. He roared, and the voice seemed much too large for the small frame from which it came.

"No," he shouted.

Frank Thomas staggered back against the wall, covering his bloody face with his left hand. Apple recovered quickly and grabbed for the arm that had sent his revolver flying. Chase grabbed at the man's shirtfront. Thomas's recovery was a bit slower, but he stepped forward, clutching once more at the left arm.

Mayor Purchase faded back against the wall behind the desk and watched the struggle. As the prisoner wrestled off his tormentors, flinging Chase to the floor before him and the others back against the wall behind, his shirt was ripped. Chase glanced up from the floor and saw the ghastly belly scar.

The thing that looked like a man reached for Apple's gun there on the floor and howled with rage and fear. He lurched forward, grabbed Chase by his shirt, lifted him from the floor, and turned and pitched him back against the office door. Chase crashed through the door, sliding along the floor of the squad room on his back.

The mayor ducked down behind the desk as Apple and Thomas started to move forward. Then he heard a fierce, inhuman growl. It echoed off the office walls and was followed by shrieks of terror from the two policemen. Purchase slowly lifted his eyes above the level of the desktop to peer out, and then he checked a scream down in his own throat.

It was like nightmares he had experienced from time to time in which he had opened his mouth to scream but no sound came out. There before him, in the middle of the office floor, loomed a monstrous grizzly bear. It stood up on its hind legs and held its forelegs wide, the long, sharp claws glistening in the artificial light. Blue rags clung here and there to the massive, hairy body. Purchase dropped back down and crawled into the knee space below the desk.

Apple and Thomas slowly staggered backward toward the door, staring almost transfixed at the great horror that now was stalking them. It swung a giant paw in their direction. Its mouth was open wide, a low growl rolling forth from deep inside, saliva dripping from the yellow teeth, the black tongue lolling out one side.

Grumbling low and menacingly in its throat, it lumbered forward, sweeping both forelegs inward in a giant semicircle. The left paw raked across the face of Apple, slinging blood and flesh into the side of Thomas's head and on across the room to splatter against the wall.

Thomas screamed hysterically as the right foreleg wrapped around behind him and drew him in close against the hairy body. He tried to scream again, but the sound was stifled in the smelly flesh against which his face was pressed, and he felt the bones in his back beginning to give way under the pressure of the powerful squeeze.

Out in the squad room, panic reigned. Chase struggled to his feet. The receptionist had already run screaming out into the street. The desk sergeant ran to Chase's side and stood in disbelief. The chief and the sergeant pulled out their revolvers and took aim, but just then the beast lifted the hapless Thomas up before him as he mauled his body.

"Don't shoot, Frank," said Chase. "Go. Go get a rifle."

The sergeant turned and ran to do as he was told. Chase held his revolver ready. Inside the office, the giant bear gave one last deadly hug and crunched the body of the man as if he'd been a bug. Then he dropped to all fours and vanished from Chase's sight. The sergeant came back with the rifle.

"Where is it?" he said.

"It's in there," said Chase. "Down on all fours. Give me that rifle."

He took the rifle from the sergeant's hands, checked to be sure that a shell was chambered, the safety off, then moved slowly to the doorway. He sidled cautiously into the doorway, his back against the jamb. He heard no noise, no growls, no moans, no breathing.

He looked in and saw no bear, only the crushed body of Frank Thomas and the bloody, faceless remains of Apple on the floor. His heart pounding hard and fast in his chest, he stepped in, then heard a quiet whimpering from behind his desk.

"Mayor?" he said. "Is that you?"

"Yes," came a wee little voice.

"Are you hurt?"

"No."

"Is that bear back there?"

"No."

"By God," said Chase in disbelief. He lowered the rifle and walked around behind the desk where he could see the mayor huddled in the knee space.

"Come on out, Mr. Mayor," he said. "It's gone."

As Purchase slowly crept out, a fat, black water beetle scurried out from under the desk on the other side and headed for the door. The desk sergeant was just coming in, and the beetle quickly changed its course to avoid the heavy footsteps of the hard-soled shoes. When the man was all the way inside the office, the beetle scampered on outside.

Chapter Seven

They sat in aluminum folding chairs with
frayed webbing that Charlie Ramos had produced from somewhere. The old man had lit a
pipeful of tobacco. Shelby wondered what the
pipe was made of. It was a short, dark pipe that
did not have the appearance of a commercially
produced product, nor did it have what Shelby
thought of as the look of an "Indian pipe." The
old man puffed quietly, and Shelby became im-
patient.

"Tell me about the bad place," he said
abruptly.

The old man's brow wrinkled slightly more with his next puff. Still he said nothing.

"Some bad things have happened there," said Shelby, "A man was killed. I need to know about that place."

The old man expelled a cloud of smoke that seemed to hover for an instant just above his head before it gradually began to dissipate into the otherwise clean, crisp desert air. Somewhere around behind the house, a dog barked.

"It's not our story," said the old man.

Shelby leaned forward in his chair, suddenly hopeful for some information.

"What?" he said.

"Some other tribe," said the old man.

"But you called it a bad place," said Shelby.

The old man nodded slowly.

"Yes," he said, "but someone else did it. Not us. It doesn't even mean anything in our language."

"What?" said Shelby. "What doesn't?"

"*Kagunyi,*" said the old man.

"*Ka-gun-yi?*" Shelby repeated.

The old man nodded slowly and puffed his pipe.

"*Kagunyi,*" said Shelby. "What is that?"

"The bad place," said the old man. "That's what they called it."

"Who?" Shelby asked. "Who called it that?"

Robert J. Conley

"That's all I know," the old man said. "It's an old story. Older than me."

He stood up then and made his slow way back to the circular door and crawled inside. Shelby stood and made a move toward the old man as if to stop him. He wanted to grab him and shake some more information out. He felt close to an answer, but suddenly it had evaded him. He thought of the childhood hiding game. *You're getting warm. You're getting warmer. Getting hot. Hot. No. Now you're getting cold again. Colder. Cold.* Shelby felt cold.

"Shit," he said.

Charlie Ramos folded up the chairs and stashed them somewhere back behind the house. Shelby stared at the hole in front of the house and realized that, even though he had been watching, he had no idea how the old man had gotten himself through it. Had he stepped through first? Gone in headfirst? Shelby couldn't imagine how the old man might look making his way into the house. He wished that he had paid closer attention. Charlie Ramos came back around the house and walked up to where Shelby stood.

"Give me a ride back to town," he said.

"Come on," said Shelby.

Shelby drove the few miles back into the reservation town in frustrated silence. Once he struck the steering wheel with the heel of his hand.

"Shit," he said.

Kay stared ahead at the road, knowing that sooner or later he'd calm down. Then she would talk to him. Shelby pulled over to the side of the road in front of the bar and grocery store and left the engine idling while Ramos jumped out of the back end. He looked back over his shoulder.

"This okay?" he asked.

Ramos walked up to the opened driver's-side window.

"You didn't learn much, did you?" he said.

"No," said Shelby. "Goddamn it."

"I think it's Cherokee," said Ramos.

"What?"

"That word," Ramos said. "*Kagunyi*. I think it's Cherokee."

"Cherokee?" Shelby said. "In California? That's crazy."

Ramos shrugged.

"At the university," he said, "there's a man who can tell you. I think. Go to the Native American Studies Department. He's the director, and he's a Cherokee. A real Cherokee. I know he's a real Cherokee, because I asked him once if his great-great-grandmother was a Cherokee princess. He said, 'No. But my great-great-grandfather was a Cherokee king.' If anyone can tell you anything about all this, he can."

"What's his name?" Shelby asked.

"Jim Green," said Ramos. "Native American Studies."

He turned and walked away.

The highway leaving the city ran parallel to the beach. He looked like a man, one of the new white men, much as he had looked before, but he had new clothes. He knew better now than to wear the blue clothes. People didn't like them. They were dangerous to wear. The men in blue were some kind of oppressive authority. He would avoid using their clothing from now on, and he would avoid the men in blue.

Back there in the city he was leaving behind him, he had gotten a fright. He would not go back there again. There must be more cities. The hard, black road had to be going somewhere. He walked along the road, the big bugs whizzing past him, going fast in both directions, none of them even running into each other.

Suddenly one of them came at him and he jumped backward, tumbling into the ditch beside the road. He came to his feet quickly, ready to fight or to run. The bug had stopped. It sat there purring. The man riding in the bug leaned toward him.

"Hey, pal," he said. "I didn't mean to scare you. You ain't hurt, are you?"

"No."

"I just thought you might want a ride."

He relaxed his stance a little. It would be interesting to ride in the bug. He could use some amusement for a change.

"Where you headed?" the man in the bug asked.

He looked ahead, not knowing where the road would take him, and he pointed down the road in the direction in which the bug was aimed and he himself had just been walking.

"That way," he said.

"Well," said the other, "hop on in."

He walked over to the bug and stood beside it. There was a hole in its side through which the man had been talking, but it was too small for him to crawl through.

"Come on," the man said.

Then the man reached across to take hold of something inside the bug, and suddenly a piece of its side swung out. He could see its insides now, see the place where sat the man and another spot where he could sit. He eased himself into that spot. *This is no bug*, he thought. *It's not alive. It's some kind of thing these people have built to ride in.*

"Close the door, will you?" the man said.

He looked at the man, then at the piece of the

side still standing wide open. *Door*. He took hold of the door and closed it.

Shelby had circled the campus once. He was about to decide arbitrarily on a street to turn into when he spotted a young man on the sidewalk. *Must be a student*, he thought. *Army-surplus fashion. Backpack*. He pulled over to the curb, and a big Lincoln Continental laying a smog cloud honked and roared around him. Kay leaned her head out the curbside window.

"Excuse me," she said in a loud voice.

The young man in the paramilitary attire stopped walking and turned his head slowly toward the pickup.

"Yeah?"

"Could you tell us where to find Native American Studies?" Kay asked.

"Oh, yeah, man," the student said. "It's way over on the other side. Just go on down here and make your right. Then go on to the next right, I mean, like you're going to go on around the whole campus, you know? Then the very next right going into the campus, you turn in there. Got it?"

"Yes," she said. "Thank you."

"Well," the student continued, "it's like in the second or third building to your left. There's a sign out in front. Says, 'Native American Stud-

ies.' Ha. Yeah. It's on the third floor. No elevator, man."

"Thank you," said Kay.

"Yeah. Thanks," said Shelby. "And we can still
handle stairs, man."

He gunned the engine. The clutch slipped,
and the Dodge lurched forward, squealing tires.

"Cool," the student said.

Shelby made three right turns and found the
building, then a parking lot.

"Come on, babe," he said.

"What if we get a parking ticket?" Kay asked,
looking back at the Dodge.

"I'll eat it," said Shelby.

They headed across the street for the building
with the Native American Studies sign out
front. According to the sign, the building also
housed the Minority Students Counselor, Black
Studies, Asian Studies, the Veterans Advisor,
and the Philosophy Department. Shelby hauled
open the heavy door.

"What are we going to find out here?" asked
Kay.

"I'm damned if I know," said Shelby. "Come
on. There's the stairs."

Shelby took the steps three at a time, while
Kay did her best to keep up with him. They
reached the third floor and began reading the
lettering on office doors as they roamed the
hallway.

"Here it is," said Shelby. He opened the door, stepped inside followed by Kay, and shut the door behind them. A young Indian woman sat behind a desk just inside the door.

"Hi," she said.

"Hello," said Shelby. "Is, uh, is Mr. Green in? We'd like to see him. Mr. Jim Green, the director."

"I'm Jim Green."

The voice came from behind Shelby. He turned to see a man standing in the doorway to an inner office. A sign over the door read, "Director." He was a man maybe in his mid-thirties, Shelby thought. He had dark hair and dark eyes, but if Shelby had seen him on the street, he might not have taken him for an Indian. His skin was dark, but it seemed to Shelby the dark of a good tan.

"Come on in," Green said.

Shelby and Kay followed Jim Green into the director's office. Shelby extended his hand.

"I'm Joe Shelby," he said, "and this is my wife, Kay."

Green shook Shelby's hand, then took hold of Kay's.

"I'm Jim Green," he said. "Glad to meet you. Have a seat."

He indicated the two visitors' chairs in the room, then sat in the chair behind his desk, an old rolltop that was cluttered with so many books and papers that its top couldn't possibly have been pulled down. The back of the desk was against the wall, so Green sat out in the middle of the room. He had to turn his chair to face his visitors.

There was a coffee cup perched precariously on the sloped top of a pile of papers and, not far from it, a dangerously overfilled ashtray. Bookshelves reached to the ceiling on two walls of the room, and they too were full. On the wall over the desk was a poster with a photograph of Sitting Bull and the quotation "God made me an Indian, but not a reservation Indian." Shelby was a little surprised at the professorial appearance of the office, but then, he wondered what he had expected.

"What can I do for you?" said Green, reaching into his shirt pocket for a cigarette.

"Do you know the word *kagunyi*?" said Shelby.

"*Kagunyi. Kagunyi,*" said Green, playing a little with stress and tone and the vowels. "Yeah. I think so. Where'd you run across it?"

"It was told to us by an old man out on the reservation near here," said Shelby. "He said it was the name of a stretch of beach down here a ways."

"That doesn't make any sense," said Green. "Not if it's the same word I'm thinking of."

"Why not?" said Kay.

"Well," said Green, exhaling smoke, "the word I'm thinking of, *kagunyi*, is an old, eastern Cherokee word. Maybe it's still pronounced that way by the eastern Cherokees. I don't know. But I'm from northeast Oklahoma. The contemporary Oklahoma Cherokee version of that same word would be *kogayi*. It means 'crow place.' Something like that."

"Crow place?" Shelby said.

"Yeah," said Green. "The place where the crows stay. Crow place. Something like that."

"Well, that's it," said Shelby. "It's got to be. Tell me about this crow place."

"It's not a real place," said Green. "I suppose the eastern Cherokees might have had a place they called by that name a long time ago. It's a place named in an old legend, a legend from hundreds, maybe thousands of years ago. It's a Cherokee word from an old Cherokee story. No local Indian would use that word—not unless he'd been reading Mooney."

"Mooney? said Shelby.

"James Mooney," Green said. "An ethnologist who recorded a bunch of the old Cherokee tales in North Carolina."

Shelby leaned forward in his chair for emphasis.

"But this old man, he said the beach was called *kagunyi*," said Shelby. "He said he didn't know what it meant because it wasn't in his language. Some other people came through here, he said, and did something and named the place. He said that's all he knows."

"But his grandson said he thought it was Cherokee," said Kay, "and he told us to come and see you."

"What was this grandson's name?" asked Green.

"Charlie," said Shelby. "Uh, Charlie Ramos."

"Yes. That's it," said Kay.

"Oh, yeah," said Green. "Charlie was a student here last year. Dropped out. What's this all about?"

Shelby leaned back and sighed. He scratched his head.

"I'm afraid it's going to sound crazy," he said.

Green shrugged.

"I'm with the Corps of Engineers," Shelby went on. Then he paused to let that bit of information sink in and to see what Green's reaction would be. Green showed no sign of reaction to Shelby's occupation or to his employer one way or the other, so Shelby continued.

"We're out here to build a recreational beach," he said. "You might have read about it. It's just down the coast from here. They're calling it Brower Recreational Beach. I'm the project engineer."

"I read about it," Green said.

"Well, this old man," Shelby said, "Indian

man, saw me in town, and he said that the beach was a bad place. I, uh, I didn't think too much about it. Then there were these two crows sitting on a pole. Out in the water. They fussed at us when we got too close. They even attacked me.

"Well, I ripped up the pole to get rid of them. I had a man with me, and we went out in a boat and pulled it up, but when it came loose, well, there was a big turmoil in the water, and then—an alligator came up. A big alligator. A giant.

"And he killed the other man. He swept him out of the boat with his tail, and he—he ate him. Right there in front of me and the rest of the crew. Then he went down, and we never saw him again.

"I went looking for the old man. The old Indian who had told me that was a bad place. We found him out on the reservation, and he said the place was called *kagunyi*, and Charlie Ramos said it was Cherokee and sent us here to see you. That's about it."

Jim Green took a last long draw on his cigarette, nearly burning the filter, then snubbed it out in the overfull ashtray.

"Are you putting me on?" he said.

"No," Shelby protested. "No, I'm not. I said it was going to sound crazy."

"You got some kind of ID," Green asked, "to show me you're really with the Corps?"

Shelby fumbled through his billfold, pulled out several cards, and handed them to Green. The girl from the desk in the outer office stepped into the doorway with a newspaper in her hand.

"Jim?" she said.

"Yeah?" he said. "What is it?"

"Here's a story 'bout that alligator," she said.

Green took the paper and read as the girl went back out to her desk. He looked up at Shelby and tossed the paper onto one of the piles already before him on the desk.

"If you're not putting me on," he said, "this is even crazier than you think."

"What do you mean?" Shelby asked.

Green spun his chair around to face a wall of books. His eyes scanned the shelves for a moment, then he pulled an old, battered book from a shelf and opened it up.

"James Mooney went to the Cherokee Reservation in North Carolina in 1887," he said. "He went to North Carolina because he thought that the Cherokees out west, in what was going to become Oklahoma, were already too assimilated in the ways of the white man for his purposes.

"You know, the government rounded up most of the Cherokees and forced them to move to what's now northeast Oklahoma. That happened in 1839. It's known as the Trail of Tears.

But a small number escaped and stayed in the hills in North Carolina. Later they got a reservation there. Those are the ones Mooney visited.

"He worked there until 1890, gathering up old stories, and he published them in 1900 in the nineteenth Annual Report of the Bureau of American Ethnology as *Myths of the Cherokee*. Let's see. Here it is. Number sixty-three. Under 'Wonder Stories.' Read it for yourself."

He handed the book to Shelby.

"That first word in the title," he said, "the first syllable is barely pronounced. Sometimes it's not pronounced at all. The *ts*, at least in my dialect in Oklahoma, is pronounced like a *j* or a *ch*. So the word sounds like *Chayi*. It's onomatopoeia. It's supposed to imitate the sound of something striking a sheet of metal, more precisely, a sheet of brass. And that's the translation of the word—brass."

Chapter Eight

Don Coleman sat at the dining table in his modest suburban house with a cold beer and a newspaper. He had been trying to read the newspaper in order to shut out the noise of the argument raging between his wife and stepdaughter in the next room, but it wasn't working. The fussing won out, so he simply sat with the newspaper in front of him, pretending, and occasionally he sipped his beer.

He had put up with this almost constant fighting, patiently, he thought, for five years now, ever since he had married Elsa Lucas Baylor, and he had cheerfully taken on the additional responsibility of raising her daughter, Judith Ann. He told himself that he had tried to be like a father to the girl, but she wouldn't let him. And he hadn't pushed, either.

She called him by his given name, Don, and she still talked about her "dad" in Ohio, often, Don was convinced, just to torment him. After Don had married Elsa, they had continued to live in Ohio for a couple of years, but Judith Ann's father had made their lives miserable. When he exercised his weekend visitation privileges, he filled the girl's head full of awful things about her mother and her new stepfather, so Coleman had found himself a job in California and moved the family. He had hoped that the distance from the father might improve things. He wanted a normal, happy family, but Judith Ann continued to talk about her "dad," continued to use the last name Baylor, and continued to call her stepfather "Don."

"I don't want to live here anymore," Judith Ann was saying.

"Where else would you go?" Elsa asked. "Where?"

"Back to Ohio," the girl said.

"Where would you live?"

"With my dad."

"Your dad has remarried," said Elsa. "You know that. His new wife doesn't want you around and in the way. We've gone through all that before. Do we have to go through it again?"

"I don't care," Judith Ann said. "I can find someplace to stay. I have friends."

"You're only sixteen years old," said Elsa, "and I have legal custody of you until you're eighteen. I'm responsible for your behavior and your well-being. Me and Don. What's wrong with you, anyway? What's wrong with your life here? Don gives you everything you want. You've got your own room, your own TV set, your own telephone."

Judith Ann turned her face to the wall. Her knees were drawn up to her chest, and she hugged them tight.

"My dad said he was going to send me some money for my birthday," she said. "Where is it?"

"How should I know?" Elsa said. "He didn't send it. That's all. It's not the first lie he ever told. Or the first promise he ever broke."

"Did you take it?"

"What?"

"Did you get my mail and take my money?"

Before she realized what she was doing, Elsa had slapped Judith Ann across the face. Tears immediately ran from the teenager's eyes, and her face flushed with anger and surprise and a little physical pain. She looked at her mother with hatred through narrow eyes.

"You bitch," she said.

Don Coleman threw down his newspaper and sprang to his feet. By the time he reached the next room, the girl had gone outside. He rushed after her, caught her by the hair, and dragged her back into the house.

"You don't talk to your mother like that," he said. He drew back his hand as if to strike her, but he stopped himself.

"Don't you touch me," said Judith Ann. "You're not my daddy."

"You're living in my house," said Coleman.

"I don't even like you."

"Judith Ann," said Elsa, "get upstairs to your room. Right now."

As Judith Ann ran for the stairs, Don Coleman went back into the dining room. He picked up his beer with a trembling hand and took a gulp.

"Goddamn it," he said. "I don't know what the hell to do. I just don't know. Just now—I almost hit her."

Elsa put her arms around Don and pulled his head down onto her shoulder.

"It's not your fault, honey," she said. "I know you've tried. Nobody could try harder. You've done everything you could. You handle things better than I do sometimes."

She paused for a moment, a pained expression on her face.

"I did hit her," she said. "I shouldn't have, but

she made me so mad accusing me of stealing her money."

Wonder Stories
63. UNTSAIYI, THE GAMBLER

Thunder lives in the west, or a little to the south of west, near the place where the sun goes down behind the water. In the old times he sometimes made a journey to the east, and once after he had come back from one of these journeys a child was born in the east who, the people said, was his son. As the boy grew up it was found that he had scrofula sores all over his body, so one day his mother said to him, "Your father, Thunder, is a great doctor. He lives far in the west, but if you can find him he can cure you."

So the boy set out to find his father and be cured. He traveled long toward the west, asking of everyone he met where Thunder lived, until at last they began to tell him that it was only a little way ahead. He went on and came to Untiguhi, on Tennessee, where lived Untsaiyi, "Brass." Now, Untsaiyi was a great gambler, and made his living that way. It was he who invented the *gatayusti* game that we play with a stone wheel and a stick. He lived on the south side of the river, and everybody who came that way he challenged to play against him. The large flat rock, with the lines and grooves where they used to roll the wheel, is still there, with the wheels themselves and the stick turned to stone. He won almost every time, because he was so tricky, so he had his house filled with all kinds of fine things. Sometimes he would lose, and then he would bet all that he had, even to his own life, but the winner got nothing for his trouble, for Untsaiyi knew how to take on different shapes, so that he always got away.

As soon as Untsaiyi saw him he asked him to stop and play awhile, but the boy said he was looking for his father, Thunder, and had no time to wait. "Well," said Untsaiyi, "he lives in the next house; you can hear him grumbling over there all the time"—he meant the Thunder—"so we may as well have a game or two before you go on." The boy said he had nothing to bet. "That's all right," said the gambler, "we'll play for your pretty spots." He said this to make the boy angry so that he would play, but still the boy said he must go first and find his father, and would come back afterward.

He went on, and soon the news came to Thunder that a boy was looking for him who claimed to be his son. Said Thunder, "I have traveled in many lands and have many children. Bring him here and we shall soon

104

know." So they brought in the boy, and Thunder showed him a seat and told him to sit down. Under the blanket on the seat were long, sharp thorns of the honey locust, with the points all sticking up, but when the boy sat down they did not hurt him, and then Thunder knew that it was his son. He asked the boy why he had come. "I have sores all over my body, and my mother told me you were my father and a great doctor, and if I came here you would cure me." "Yes," said his father, "I am a great doctor, and I'll soon fix you."

There was a large pot in the corner, and he told his wife to fill it with water and put it over the fire. When it was boiling, he put in some roots, then took the boy and put him in with them. He let it boil a long time until one would have thought that the flesh was boiled from the poor boy's bones, and then told his wife to take the pot and throw it into the river, boy and all. She did as she was told, and threw it into the water, and ever since there is an eddy there that we call Untiguhi, "Pot-in-the-water." A service tree and a calico bush grew on the bank above. A great cloud of steam came up and made streaks and blotches on their bark, and it has been so to this day. When the steam cleared away she looked over and saw the boy clinging to the roots of the service tree where they hung down into the water, but now his skin was all clean. She helped him up the bank, and they went back to the house. On the way she told him, "When we go in, your father will put a new dress on you, but when he opens his box and tells you to pick out your ornaments be sure to take them from the bottom. Then he will send for his other sons to play ball against you. There is a honey locust tree in front of the house, and as soon as you begin to get tired strike at that and your father will stop the play, because he does not want to lose the tree."

When they went into the house, the old man was pleased to see the boy looking so clean, and said, "I knew I could cure those spots. Now we must dress you." He brought out a fine suit of buckskin, with belt and head-dress, and had the boy put them on. Then he opened a box and said, "Now pick out your necklace and bracelets." The boy looked, and the box was full of all kinds of snakes gliding over each other with their heads up. He was not afraid, but remembered what the woman had told him, and plunged his hand to the bottom and drew out a great rattlesnake and put it around his neck for a necklace. He put down his hand again four times and drew up four copperheads and twisted them around his wrists and ankles. Then his father gave him a war club and said, "Now you must play a ball game with your two elder brothers. They live beyond here in the Darkening Land, and I have sent for them." He said a ball game, but he meant that the boy must fight for his life. The young men came, and they were both older and stronger than the boy, but he was not afraid and fought against them. The thunder rolled and the lightning flashed at every stroke, for they were the young Thunders, and the boy himself was Lightning. At last he was tired from defending himself alone against two, and pretended to aim a blow at the honey locust tree. Then his father stopped the fight, because he was afraid the lightning would split the tree, and he saw that the boy was brave and strong.

The boy told his father how Untsaiyi had dared him to play, and had even offered to play for the spots on his skin. "Yes," said Thunder, "he is a great gambler and makes his living that way, but I will see that you win." He brought a small cymling gourd with a hole bored through the neck, and tied it on the boy's wrist. Inside the gourd there was a string of beads, and one end hung out from a hole in the top, but there was no end to the string inside. "Now," said his father, "go back the way you came, and as soon as he sees you he will want to play for the beads. He is very hard to beat, but this time he will lose every game. When he cries out for a drink, you will know he is getting discouraged, and then strike the rock with your war club and water will come, so that you can play on without stopping. At last he will bet his life, and lose. Then send at once for your brothers to kill him, or he will get away, he is so tricky."

The boy took the gourd and his war club and started east along the road by which he had come. As soon as Untsaiyi saw him he called to him, and when he saw the gourd with the bead string hanging out he wanted to play for it. The boy drew out the string, but there seemed to be no end to it, and he kept on pulling until enough had come out to make a circle all around the playground. "I will play one game for this much against your stake," said the boy, "and when that is over we can have another game."

They began the game with the wheel and stick, and the boy won. Untsaiyi did not know what to think of it, but he put up another stake and called for a second game. The boy won again, and so they played on until noon, when Untsaiyi had lost nearly everything he had and was about discouraged. It was very hot, and he said, "I am thirsty," and wanted to stop long enough to get a drink. "No," said the boy, and struck the rock with his club so that water came out, and they had a drink. They played on until Untsaiyi had lost all of his buckskins and beaded work, his eagle feathers and ornaments, and at last offered to bet his wife. They played, and the boy won her. Then Untsaiyi was desperate and offered to stake his life. "If I win I kill you, but if you win you may kill me." They played, and the boy won.

"Let me go and tell my wife," said Untsaiyi, "so that she will receive her new husband, and then you may kill me." He went into the house, but it had two doors, and although the boy waited long, Untsaiyi did not come back. When at last he went to look for him he found that the gambler had gone out the back way and was nearly out of sight going east.

The boy ran to his father's house and got his brothers to help him. They brought their dog—the Horned Green Beetle—and hurried after the gambler. He ran fast and was soon out of sight, and they followed as fast as they could. After a while they met an old woman making pottery and asked her if she had seen Untsaiyi, and she said she had not. "He came this way," said the brothers. "Then he must have passed in the night," said the old woman, "for I have been here all day." They were about to take another road when the

Beetle, which had been circling about in the air above the old woman, made a dart at her and struck her on the forehead, and it rang like brass—*untsaiyi*! Then they knew it was Brass and sprang at him, but he jumped up in his right shape and was off, running so fast that he was soon out of sight again. The Beetle had struck so hard that some of the brass rubbed off, and we can see it on the beetle's forehead yet.

They followed and came to an old man sitting by the trail, carving a stone pipe. They asked him if he had seen Brass pass that way and he said no, but again the Beetle—which could know Brass under any shape—struck him on the forehead so that it rang like metal, and the gambler jumped up in his right form and was off again before they could hold him. He ran east until he came to the great water; then he ran north until he came to the edge of the world and had to turn again to the west. He took every shape to throw them off the track, but the Green Beetle always knew him, and the brothers pressed him so hard that at last he could go no more and they caught him just as he reached the edge of the great water where the sun goes down.

They tied his hands and feet with a grape-vine and drove a long stake through his breast, and planted it far out in the deep water. They set two crows on the end of the pole to guard it and called the place Kagunyi, "Crow Place." But Brass never died, and cannot die until the end of the world, but lies there always with his face up. Sometimes he struggles under the water to get free, and sometimes the beavers, who are his friends, come and gnaw at the grapevine to release him. Then the pole shakes and the crows at the top cry *Ka! Ka! Ka!* and scare the beavers away.

Chapter Nine

"So what's your name, pal? Mine's Carl Stokes. Call me Carl or call me Stokes. Hell, it don't matter to me."

Stokes twisted his right arm to offer a handshake to his passenger while keeping his left hand on the wheel, his eyes on the road.

"My name is Brass," said the passenger.

They shook hands, and Stokes was a bit disgusted at the limp grip of the man who called himself Brass.

"Brass," he said with a sneer. "That's a kind of an unusual name, ain't it? Huh? I don't be-

lieve I ever run across anyone by that name before. Never. Where you come from, Brass?"

"Oh, around here," Brass said.

"You come from 'around here,' you're heading 'that way.' You got that weird name, and you
got a funny handshake, but you don't seem like
no faggot to me. Hell, you're some kind of mysterious, ain't you?"

"I guess so," said Brass.

Brass didn't like the questions that Stokes
was asking him. He didn't want the blue-suited
authorities to find him again, and he was in-
tensely aware of being in a totally alien
environment. He wondered what had become
of all the kind of people he remembered from
ages past. He wished that he could find them,
but they must have all vanished—or changed.
He wished that this man would stay quiet and
just guide his machine. *Car*, he had heard it
called. *Car*. He must remember *car*.

"Hell," said Stokes, "it don't matter none to
me. I done some things in my time I'd just as
soon nobody ever knows about. Know what I
mean?"

"Yes," said Brass, and he thought, *Your time
on this earth, you foolish man, has been very
short, and you know very little*.

"You know," said Stokes, "I wouldn't even
have picked you up in the first place, but it looks
to me like it's fixing to rain tonight. There's a

hell of a lot of weirdos out on the roads these days. You never know what the hell you're picking up anymore, but still, I hate to see a man stuck out in the damn rain on foot."

"Thank you," said Brass.

"I'm going fishing tonight, myself," Stokes rambled on. "That's where I'm going. My old lady's in the hospital fixing to have another kid. I feel just a little bit guilty about going out fishing all night, her in the hospital like that and all, but, hell, I was there the last time, and all I done was just get in the way."

Brass smiled. He didn't know what *hospital* was, but he was glad that Stokes had started talking about himself and had stopped asking him difficult and troublesome questions. Stokes leaned forward with a grunt, reached under the seat beneath himself, and brought up a large drinking glass. He held it up for Brass to see.

"You see this?" he said. "This here's my beer-drinking glass. I bet you I fill this son of a bitch up a hundred times tonight."

Bet, Brass thought. Passionate memories of long ago swept through his mind at the sound of the word. He would like to bet, but he had no stake, and besides that, he wasn't at all sure that he understood the man's bet.

"I see it," said Brass. He didn't know *beer*, and he didn't know *son of a bitch*. Stokes's conversation was a great puzzle to him, even with his linguistic gift. Did the man think that he couldn't see? That had seemed like a stupid question.

"Brass, huh?" said Stokes. "Just what the hell kind of a name is Brass, anyhow?"

"It's just my name," said Brass. He didn't think that it would do to tell the man that it was also the primary material from which his body was composed, including the hard shell just underneath the outer layer of humanlike skin. Inside the shell of brass, of course, he had blood and guts just like humans, but when he was hurt, he also had an amazing ability to heal quickly.

"Yeah?" Stokes said. "Hell, that's all right. I don't know what the hell kind of name Stokes is either. I think maybe it's English, but I don't really know. Now, Hans and Fritz and things like that are German. I know them. O'Haras and O'Connells and such are Irish. And Polanskys and stuff, they're Polack. One-hung-low, that's Chinese."

Stokes burst into sudden laughter, and Brass wondered what was so funny. He suspected that he must have missed a joke. The situation was beginning to feel much too awkward for Brass's comfort. Stokes stopped laughing and gave Brass a slightly disgusted look.

"Anyhow," he said, "I don't know about

Stokes and Brass. Just good old American, I guess."

"I guess," said Brass. He didn't know *English* or *German* or *Polack* or *Chinese* or *American*, but he didn't think that it would be wise just then to point out that deficiency to Stokes.

"You got a wife?" Stokes asked.

"I did have," said Brass. "Once. A long time ago."

Brass had not thought about his wife and home for—what? Centuries? Memories long lost in the back of his mind inched their way painfully forward. He tried to remember what she had looked like, but he could not. He wondered how long she had been dead. He tried to recall the feel of her touch and the more intimate details of their relationship, and an unfamiliar stirring in his loins startled him.

"Divorced?" Stokes asked.

Brass did not know *divorced*. He looked at Stokes, a puzzled expression on his face.

"Well, hell," said Stokes, "don't tell me, then. I don't really give a shit. Just trying to make conversation, that's all. Goddamn. I never seen such a clam. Shit. Give a man a fucking ride, you'd think he could be just a little bit friendly."

They rode on a few miles in uncomfortable silence. Stokes was obviously pouting. *Just keep quiet*, thought Brass. *All I want from you is a ride in your car to—someplace*. He thought about the way the people in town had ignored him until the men in blue had seen him in the blue suit he had conjured to go with his first new human form. He had seen it on the first people he saw, and therefore his mind had copied it. But it had been a mistake. He hoped that the clothes he had on this time wouldn't offend anyone. He longed for another town and for the anonymity of these modern, peculiar crowds of people.

"I don't give a flying fuck if you murdered your wife," said Stokes. "Hell, I ain't prying."

"I didn't kill her," said Brass, and he thought of the number of times he had used her as a gambling stake, but then, he thought, that was all right, because he had never really given her over to anyone. Never, that is, except for that last time. *I wonder,* he thought, *did he go back and take her, that Lightning boy? After he tied me up, him and his brothers? After they stabbed me through and pinned me to the ocean floor? What did she think? How did she feel? Did she like him better than me? What he did to her?* He felt the stirring again, and it made him angry.

"Don't ask me any more questions," he said. "I don't like them."

"Hell," said Stokes, "I'll just pull this thing over the next chance I get and kick your ass on out of here. You won't have to bother with me no more. No sir. No more questions."

A big eighteen-wheeler pulled up alongside the car to pass, and Stokes's attention was drawn to it for a moment. When he looked forward again, his peripheral vision picked up a strange and shocking image. He turned his head to the right, and there sat, not the man he had picked up on the road, but an old, wrinkled Indian woman, a shawl wrapped about her head and shoulders. She smiled a gap-toothed grin at him.

"I'll bet you your car," she said, "that you don't know how I got here."

Stokes gasped out loud. In his shock, he lost control of the car, and in his desperate attempt to regain it and at the same time keep a watch on the mysterious figure beside him, he ran off the road into the low median in the center of the divided highway. The car bumped to a halt, and the engine died. Unbelieving and horror stricken, Stokes looked at the grinning old woman as he fumbled desperately behind himself for the door handle.

"Will you make the bet?" she said.

"Get out of here," he shouted. "Go on. Get the hell out of my car."

The old woman lifted her right hand, letting the shawl drop away from it to reveal an index finger that grew into an eighteen-inch, sharply tapered spike, much like an awl or an ice pick. She cackled. Stokes screamed. The old one jabbed suddenly with her right hand, driving the awl-finger upward into the soft flesh just under Stokes's chin. His scream was stifled as the end of the sharp spear came out the top of his head, causing blood to squirt upward onto the headliner of the car. Stokes quivered for an instant, then went limp.

"You lose," the old woman said, "and the car is mine now."

Shelby handed the book back to Jim Green. For a long moment he sat silent.

"Well?" said Green.

"Well, can I read it?" asked Kay.

"Oh, sure," said Green. "I'm sorry."

He opened the book back to the proper page and handed it over to Kay.

"Number sixty-three," he said.

"Thank you," she said, and she started to read.

"You, uh, you can't expect me to believe that story is real, can you?" said Shelby. "I mean, it's a fairy tale. You think that it's real, and he's been out there all this time? That—Brass? Alive? Do you? And then I came along and pulled up the pole and turned him loose? He turned into a giant alligator and ate Bud? Is that what you think? Come on. That's—that's crazy, that's what it is."

"If I remember correctly," said Green, "that's

just what you told me your story was going to sound like when you came in here."

Shelby stood up and paced the floor. He glanced out at the receptionist at her desk and thought that she was working much too hard at appearing not to have been listening to what was going on in Green's office. He wanted to tell her so, but he didn't. He turned back to Green instead.

"Yeah," he said. "That's right. I said that. I did. I said it's going to sound crazy. But a man made out of brass? A man that can't die? That can take any shape he wants? Just like that? No. No, there's got to be some other explanation."

"I think so too," said Green, "but you asked me about the word *kagunyi*. You told me about the crows and the pole and the alligator and the boiling water and the bad place. All I've done is to show you the one story I know about that all that seems to relate to."

"Damn," said Shelby. "It does all fit, but it's just too goddamned insane."

"It doesn't really all fit," said Green. "Not quite. The story is a little ambiguous. It makes references to some local North Carolina sites, yet it seems to imply that Brass and Thunder lived near the West Coast."

"Yeah?" said Shelby. "Well, now, how do you explain that?"

Green gave a casual shrug.

"Who knows how old that tale is?" he said. "How many times might it have been told and retold before Mooney ever heard it in the nineties? I don't know, either, which of Mooney's informants told the story to him, and whether it was told to him in English or in Cherokee. If it was told to him in Cherokee, then who translated it, and how good a job of translating was done? There are a number of questions and a number of possible explanations for the ambiguities."

Kay closed the book and handed it gingerly back to Jim Green.

"Then you don't think it could be true?" she asked.

"It was Shakespeare who wrote, 'There are more things in heaven and earth than are dreamt of in your philosophy,'" said Green. "He was a white man."

"No," said Shelby. "No way. Hell no."

"Mr. Shelby," said Green, "I'd like to go back with you and look this place over. This *kogayi*. Do you mind?"

"You said you didn't believe this shit," said Shelby.

"I don't," said Green, "but I have an open mind. I'd still like to go."

"Why not, Joe?" Kay said. "What can it hurt?"

"Ah, hell," said Shelby. "I don't mind. Come on, then. Let's go."

Chapter Ten

The sun set on Brass as he sat in the car beside what had been Carl Stokes. A few vehicles sped by on the road above, but none of the drivers noticed the car down below in the median, or if they did, they didn't pay any attention to it. Brass was himself again, and he sat in the car trying to decide what his next move should be.

He decided that he wanted the car; therefore, he had to dispose of Stokes. He remembered that Stokes had reached for something on the inside of the door in order to open it. He found a handle, tried it, and broke it off. He found another one and pulled on it. The door opened. He stepped out onto the grass and watched the road.

A car drove by with its lights on. He had not seen the lights before. *They can see in the dark,* he thought. He reached into the car and across the front seat to grasp the body of Stokes by its right arm, and he pulled it out, dropping it into the grass. Then he dragged it around behind the car.

He moved back to the open door and got back inside the car, scooting across the seat to sit behind the wheel. The wheel was the thing that Stokes had used to guide the car. He had seen Stokes, too, press the things on the floor with his feet. He could make the car go, he thought. He grasped the wheel in both hands, and he mashed the things on the floor with his feet. The car did not respond. He gave the wheel a violent jerk. The car seemed to be dead.

"Go!" he shouted.

Nothing happened. He thought back, trying to remember everything he had seen Stokes do to the car. He shook the wheel in his massive hands, and he stamped the things on the floor with his feet. Ah, yes, when Brass had first gotten in, Stokes had moved the stick that stuck out just behind the wheel. Brass grabbed the stick and shoved it upward. Still nothing.

"Go! Go! Go!" he shouted angrily.

Still the car did not respond. He roared in anger and banged his fist into the center of the wheel. The car responded with a loud and unearthly blast of noise. Brass yelled in fright and jumped, sitting there behind the wheel. He crawled hastily back out, again through the passenger-side door, backed several paces away from the car, and stood there in the darkness.

His inability to make the car go frustrated him enormously. He was beginning to be angry at the car. After it had howled at him when he struck it, he was no longer certain that the thing was not alive. Perhaps after all it was a big bug that these strange people had somehow managed to tame.

Up on the road one of the very large cars with lots of wheels roared by. It had more lights than did the car that had passed by earlier, and some of them were red and some were yellow. Brass turned and hit Stokes's car with the flats of both his hands, causing it to rock in its tracks. It did not howl at him this time.

He would have to start walking again. He would have to go back up on the road. Maybe someone else would stop and give him a ride. If so, he would not be afraid when the car stopped beside him this time. He would know how to open the door. He would have to look like one of the new white men again.

But first he would do something about his

hunger. It had been some time since he had eaten, and his stomach was beginning to rumble. He thought of Stokes, lying back there, going to waste. Human flesh was not really to his taste, not when he was himself, so he changed himself into a large buzzard and settled down to a sumptuous feast.

Judith Ann Baylor walked along the shoulder of the coast highway. She had no destination in mind, not really. Her goal was to get away. She vaguely thought about getting back to Ohio, but that was a long way, and getting there would take some planning. Judith Ann didn't even know what highway would lead her in the direction of Ohio, so for now she was just getting away, just going, just being free.

It was beginning to get cold, and she was afraid, out on the highway alone in the dark of night, but she was also determined that she would not go back home. *Home*, she thought. The word disgusted her. Coleman's house was not her home, but then, her daddy's house with his new wife in it now—that wouldn't be home either.

Judith Ann realized that she no longer had a place she could call home, and she started to cry. That made her mad. She wiped her eyes. She concentrated on her hatred. She hated Don Coleman, and though she had never seen the woman, she hated her new stepmother in Ohio, and she hated both her parents for having created the intolerable situation in which she found herself.

A Thunderbird roared past her on the highway, slowed ahead a little ways, and pulled over onto the shoulder to stop. Then it began backing up toward her. A ride, she thought. She started to run to meet the car. *A brand-new T-bird. Cool.* When she was even with the front passenger door, the window started down.

The driver, a man with gray hair around his ears but none on top of his head, sat comfortably behind the wheel poking a button with a finger of his left hand. He looked at her and smiled.

"You want a ride, girlie?" he asked.

"Yeah, man," said Judith Ann.

She opened the door and jumped in. As she closed the door, the window started back up. Then, with the press of another button, the door was locked.

"Nice car," said Judith Ann.

"Glad you like it," said the driver. "How far you going?"

"I'm going as far as you'll take me, mister," she said. "Ain't going no place special. I'm leaving some shit behind me. That's all."

She scrunched herself back into the plush seat.

"Call me Leon," said the driver.

"Huh?"

"I said, 'Call me Leon.' Don't call me mister."

"Oh," Judith Ann said. "Okay . . . Leon."

"I know I'm old enough to be your father," Leon said, "maybe even your grandfather, but that doesn't mean I have to act that old. Does it?"

Judith Ann shrugged.

"No," she said. "I guess not."

"Or that you have to treat me like I'm old?" Leon added.

"Naw."

"How old are you?" Leon asked.

Judith Ann squinted her eyes at him.

"How old are you?" she asked.

"Come on," said Leon. "I asked first."

"All right," she said. "I'm eighteen."

Leon laughed out loud.

"What's so fucking funny?" Judith Ann said.

"You're not eighteen," said Leon. "I'd say more like fifteen. I'd say you're a runaway. Am I right?"

"Hey," Judith Ann said. "Just pull over and let me out of here. Okay? It's none of your fucking business how old I am anyway."

"Calm down," said Leon. "Just take it easy. I don't care one way or the other. I'm not going to turn you in."

Judith Ann sat quietly while Leon drove another mile or so down the road.

"I'm sixteen," she said. "And I'm running away from home."

"That's okay with me, kiddo," Leon said. "Hell, look, I'm helping you. I could get in trouble for that, you know?"

"All right," she said. "I'm sorry I yelled at you. Thanks for the ride."

"It's okay," said Leon. "And I'm sixty."

"I don't mind," said Judith Ann.

"Why should you?" Leon said. "You know what they say? The older the violin, the sweeter the music."

"Yeah," said Judith Ann. "Speaking of music . . ."

"Help yourself," said Leon.

Judith Ann leaned forward and turned on the radio, then began searching for a station to her liking. She found one playing hard rock, tuned it in carefully, and turned up the volume. Leon winced but kept quiet. He drove on through three songs and the advertisements in between. Then he pulled over into a roadside lot. The sign read, "Rest Stop. No Facilities." There were no other cars there.

"What are you doing?" Judith Ann asked.

"I'm a little tired," said Leon. "Have to rest my eyes awhile."

"I can drive," she said.

"No," he said. "I think I'll just rest for a short while. Then we'll go on. You hungry?"

"I guess so," she said.

"There's a place to eat not far from here," he said. "We'll get a couple of hamburgers or a pizza or something. How's that sound?"

"I don't want anybody to see me," said Judith Ann.

"I'll get it and bring it out to you," Leon said.

"I don't have any money," she said.

"That's okay, kid," Leon said. "I'll buy."

Leon settled back into the seat. He stretched his right arm out casually and let it fall on the headrest of the passenger seat back. The radio dj started up another record, and the music vibrated the T-bird's dashboard. Beads of sweat formed on Leon's high forehead, and he began to breathe heavily. He felt his heart pounding in his chest, and he felt something even more basic farther below.

He caught Judith Ann behind the head with his right hand and pulled her to him. Suddenly his mouth was on hers, mashing, slobbering. He forced his tongue between her lips. She struggled, trying to cry out. She twisted her face away from the unwanted kisses, and Leon's tongue lapped at her cheek and her ear and her neck.

"Let me go," she screamed.

The rock music continued to pound in the

space inside the car, as Leon's left hand shoved itself rudely up the inside of Judith Ann's thighs and pressed hard into her crotch. His face was still mashed against hers.

"Come on, baby," he said. "Don't fight me. It's okay. You'll like it. Come on."

He grabbed her right hand with his left and pulled on it, pressing it between his own legs, forcing her to feel the throbbing there.

"The older the violin, the sweeter the music," he whispered harshly into her ear.

With all the strength she could summon, Judith Ann wrenched her right arm loose and slapped the side of Leon's head, catching him solidly on the ear.

"Ow," he yelled.

He let her go and clutched at the side of his head, while she moved as far away from him as she could and fumbled at the door handle.

"You bastard," she said. "Let me out of here."

"Why'd you do that?" said Leon. "You didn't have to hit me."

"Open the door!"

"What's the matter?" he asked. "You want me to pay you? How much do you want?"

"Unlock the door, you smelly old fart," she screamed.

Leon pressed the button to unlock the door, and Judith Ann jerked the handle and jumped out of the car. Leaving the door standing wide, she backed off toward the weeds at the far edge of the parking area.

"Do you think I'd want to fuck you?" she shouted. "Even for your money? You shit. You old prick. Get the hell away from me."

"All right," said Leon. "All right. I'm going. And I'm calling the cops too. They'll find you, and they'll take you back where you came from. Or better yet, they'll put you in an institution where you belong, you little bitch."

He started the engine and stomped on the gas, squealing tires as he turned back out onto the highway, the door swinging shut from the force of the wind created by the motion and speed of the car. Judith Ann stood alone in the darkness watching the red taillights of the Thunderbird get smaller.

"Shitass," she screamed.

She wiped at the tears in her eyes and the drool on her face with her shirtsleeve. She took a few deep breaths and decided to resume her walk. *What if he does call the cops?* She wondered if she should leave the road and walk across fields. If she did that, she was afraid, she would get lost. There was a noise behind her, like a movement of someone or something in the weeds. She felt a lump of fear in her throat. She thought about running. Then she heard the voice.

"I have a car," it said.

Robert J. Conley

The voice was calm and pleasant enough. She turned slowly to face its owner. She couldn't see him clearly for the darkness and the blur that was still in her eyes from the tears, but he seemed to be a nice-looking young man. He couldn't be any worse than that bastard, Leon, she thought.

"Who are you?" she asked.

"My name is Brass," he said. "Don't be afraid. I won't hurt you. I have a car."

"What are you doing out here?" she asked.

"Walking," he said. "What are you doing out here?"

Judith Ann laughed.

"Walking," she said. "If you have a car, why are we both out here walking?"

"I can't make it go," said Brass. "I don't know how. Do you know?"

"I ain't a mechanic," she said.

"Mechanic?" said Brass. "I don't know—mechanic."

Judith Ann walked slowly toward Brass. Something was wrong with him, she thought. *Retarded, maybe.* Yet somehow he didn't seem to her to be harmful. She wasn't afraid.

"How did your car stop?" she asked.

"There was a man in it," said Brass, "making it go, and he left. I can't make it go."

"Do you mean you can't drive?" she said, emphasizing the last word.

132

"Drive?" he said.

"Where is your car?" Judith Ann said.

"This way."

Brass led Judith Ann a little way down the dark highway, across two lanes, and down into the median to where the car sat.

"Wow," she said. "This is an old one. What is it? A 'fifty Ford?"

Brass shrugged.

"It's a car," he said.

"I bet it's a stick," said Judith Ann.

"It's a car," said Brass.

Judith Ann opened the door and got in behind the wheel.

"The dome light even works," she said. "Hey! No! It's an old automatic. All right."

She leaned forward, looking for the key, and she noticed the registration tag strapped to the steering column. *Carl Stokes. He said his name is Brass. Goddamn it*, she thought. *He stole it. What the hell? I don't give a shit. Why should I?*

She placed the gearshift lever in neutral and tried the key. The engine roared to a start, then hummed evenly as she let up on the gas pedal.

"Get in," she said.

Brass got in on the passenger's side and closed the door. Then Judith Ann shut the other door, and the interior light went out. Brass looked around, puzzled at the disappearance of the light. Judith Ann found the button for the headlights and pulled it out, illuminating their path ahead.

"This one can see at night too," said Brass.

"Let's see if we can get this thing out of here," Judith Ann said.

She shifted into low and pressed the gas pedal. Bumping and lurching, the Ford climbed up the slope of the median with no real trouble, and then they were racing on down the highway. Brass smiled.

"You made it go," he said. "Good."

"Where are you going?" she asked him.

Brass shrugged. "I don't know," he said.

"I don't know where I'm going either," Judith Ann said. "Maybe we can go there together."

Brass laughed. He thought that was a good joke. He liked this girl. He was glad he had found her. Then he remembered the man she had been shouting at, the man who had shouted back at her and threatened her.

"That man back there," he said. "He said someone was going to get you."

"That old son of a bitch," she said. "He's going to call the cops."

"Cops?"

"The police," said Judith Ann. "The boys in blue. You know?"

"The men in the blue clothes?" said Brass.

"Yeah, man," she said.

"I know them," said Brass. "Cops."

"Cops," she said.

"Will they come after you?" he asked.

"I guess they will," she said. "If he calls them."

"They don't like me either," Brass said thoughtfully. "Maybe we should stop him before he calls them."

Chapter Eleven

"There's his car," said Judith Ann as she whipped the old Ford off the highway and into the gravel parking lot of a roadside café.

"Where?" said Brass.

"Right here beside us," she said. She looked over at Brass and smiled as she pulled in beside the Thunderbird and parked. Brass looked around.

"Where is the man?" he asked.

"He must be inside getting something to eat," she said, "or making a phone call."

"What's a phone call?" Brass said.

"Shit, man," Judith Ann said. "Are you for real? A telephone, you know?"

"No," said Brass. "I don't know—telephone."

"Well," said Judith Ann, "it's—it's a way he can call the cops, okay?"

"Yes," he said. "Well, I'd better go in there and stop him, then."

Brass pulled the door handle, and the door popped open, lighting the interior of the car. Judith Ann grabbed his arm.

"Wait," she said. "Shut the door."

He did, and he looked at her.

"Why?" he asked.

"Listen," she said, and there was frustration in the tone of her voice. "We got to talk this thing over first. You can't just go in there and—well, we got to talk about it."

"Okay," said Brass.

Judith Ann knew that Brass intended to kill Leon. That could be his only intent. She figured that he had already killed Carl Stokes in order to steal the Ford. There were dark stains on the seatback, the door panel, and the headliner that could be blood.

And Brass had said that it was his car, but the car was registered to Stokes. Brass was a killer. She was certain of that. She thought that probably she should get the hell away from him. She could send him on inside to get Leon—he was ready to do it—and run off in the Ford while he was inside the café.

She could, yet somehow she didn't want to. She liked Brass. He was cute, she thought, and he was nice to her. Besides, there was something wrong with him, and he needed her, or somebody, to look after him. No telling what he might get himself into if she ran out on him. So what if he'd killed someone? Stokes was probably a shit anyway—like Leon. They deserved it. She was frightened, but it was an exciting kind of fright. She liked it. She made up her mind.

"Listen," she said, "the cops are probably looking for this car by now. We ought to get another one."

"All right," he said.

"We can stop Leon from calling the cops," she said, "and get his car, but how are we going to do it?"

"Leon is the man?" Brass asked.

"Yeah," she said, "Leon. That's his name."

"I'll stop Leon," Brass said.

"Wait a minute," said Judith Ann. "Jeez. You can't just go in there and get him just like that. They'll see you in there."

Brass thought for a moment, and he had made a plan. It was a good one.

"I can do it," he said calmly, "and they won't see me either."

"How the hell can you do that?" Judith Ann asked. "Can you make yourself invisible or what?"

Brass liked the girl, but he didn't think that he should tell her his secrets. Not just yet, anyway. That might scare her away, and he wanted her to stay.

"I can do it," he said. "Never mind how."

"Well, even if you can," said Judith Ann, "we need his car keys to steal his car, and as long as we're going that far, we ought to get his money too. You got any money? I ain't got any."

"Money?" said Brass.

"Oh, no," she said, throwing her head back and putting a hand to her forehead. "Don't tell me you don't know what money is either."

"But I don't," he said.

"Oh, shit, man."

"I'm sorry," said Brass.

"No, look, it's okay," she said. "Look. Money's to buy things with. We need money to buy things, to get food to eat, gas to make the car go, whatever. We just need money, man. Everything costs money. We can't go any place or do anything without it."

"I thought you made the car go," Brass said.

"Well, I did, but it needs gas too," she said. "And gas costs money. I know. Don't even say it. You don't have to tell me. You don't know what gas is either. Well, it's like food for the car, okay? And it costs money, like everything else."

"Okay," said Brass. "Does Leon have money?"

"Yeah," said Judith Ann. "Anyone who drives a car like that has got money."

"Then we'll get his money," Brass said, "and his—what else did you say?"

"His car keys," she said. "Like this."

Judith Ann pulled the keys out of the Ford's ignition and dangled them in front of Brass. He studied them for a moment.

"Okay," he said.

He thought about the plan he had made to kill Leon, but he realized that with that plan, he wouldn't be able to get the keys or the money. He didn't even know what money looked like. He might be able to get the keys, but Judith Ann would have to get the money.

"Listen," said Judith Ann. "I got it. Let's just wait here. He'll be coming out of there pretty soon now. When he comes out here, you can get him right there at his car, and then we'll get the keys and the money and get the hell out of here."

Brass thought about the suggestion for a moment. He could still use his original plan after all. He would just do it outside instead of in. *Good*, he thought. It would be even better that way. Judith Ann was smart. He liked that about her.

"Yes. That's a good plan," he said. "I'll go out now and get ready."

"Where are you going?" said Judith Ann. She felt a moment of panic.

"Just over there," he said. "Okay?"

He pointed vaguely toward the big Thunder-bird, then opened the door and got out. He gave Judith Ann a reassuring look, shut the door behind himself, and walked around to the opposite side of Leon's car. Then he crouched down low, out of sight of Judith Ann as well as anyone who might be looking from inside the building.

At the counter inside the café, Leon was just finishing a last cup of coffee. He had eaten a hamburger and a piece of apple pie with cheese on top. The waitress had given him a funny look when he'd asked for the cheese. Where the hell had she been all her life, anyway? he thought. Stupid cow. He had considered making the phone call to the police to get even with the damned kid, but then he had decided against it. After all, she was just sixteen years old. Anyhow, that's what she said.

If he set the cops on her, she might tell them that he'd tried to rape her or something, and he sure didn't need that kind of mess in his life. He shuddered when he thought of the reactions he'd get from his family and from the office personnel if anything like that got around about him. *Damn stupid little slut*, he thought.

He gulped down the rest of the coffee, stood up and fumbled in his trouser pocket for change, found a quarter, and tossed it onto the counter for a tip. The damned waitress didn't deserve any more than that, he thought. He picked up the check and walked over to the cash register, where he paid with a bill from his wallet.

"Let me have a receipt," he said.

The cashier tore the bottom off the check and handed it to him. He tucked it in the wallet and stuffed the wallet back in his hip pocket. He glanced once more at the pay phone on the wall and hesitated just a moment. *Nah*, he told himself. *To hell with it*. Then he went into the men's room.

Judith Ann could see Leon through the large window on the front of the café. She watched him get up from the counter and go to the cash register, and she saw him go into the rest room. *He'll be coming out any minute*, she thought. She looked around for Brass, but he was nowhere in sight. *Goddamn him. He's run out on me. The chickenshit. The stupid retard shit*. She scrunched herself down low in the seat to avoid being seen as she watched Leon walk out into the parking lot.

* * *

On the passenger side of the big T-bird, a large brown spider crawled up the window glass and then onto the roof. It moved quickly and deliberately to the other side and down to the door handle. Soon the man came. He walked in between the two cars. *This must be the one. The one I must kill.* The man paused for a moment, reaching into a pocket of his clothing. Then he pulled out car keys. The spider was proud of its recognition of the object. The hand with the keys moved toward the door handle, and the spider jumped.

"Ah."

Leon yelled and dropped his keys as he felt the furry creature land on his hand. Even before he could react to slap at it, he felt the awful sting. Then he slapped, but it was gone. It was running up his sleeve. He slapped again.

"Ah."

Damn, his head was hurting. Then he felt another bite, this one on the side of his neck. He screamed and slapped at the pain, but the creature responsible for it had run down the back of his coat, dropped to the ground, and run under the car. Leon still slapped. His hand felt swollen, and then his neck, and then his head.

"Oh, God," he said.

He turned back toward the café to go for help, but he suddenly felt paralyzed. His head was splitting with pain. His throat felt closed up. He couldn't breathe. He dropped to his knees in the parking lot, crying, whimpering, trying to suck in air, trying to call for help. Then he fell forward.

Brass jerked open the driver's-side door of the 'fifty Ford, and Judith Ann jumped and screamed.

"Come on," he said.

He held up Leon's car keys.

"I got the keys," he said. "Go get the money."

"But he's—"

"He can't do anything," said Brass. "Let's go before the cops come."

Judith Ann gathered all her courage, crawled out of the car, and ran to where Leon lay jerking on the ground. She found his billfold and took it. She thought about reaching into his front trouser pocket for change but rejected that idea. She ran back to Brass waiting at the T-bird.

"Give me the keys," she said. "Let's get the fuck out of here."

Chapter Twelve

As Shelby passed the office of Mayor Purchase, he knew that something was wrong, something more had happened in his absence. There were two heavily armed policemen standing guard outside the mayor's door. Shelby was anxious to park. He wanted to fill the chief of police in on what he had discovered, he wanted to find out what had occurred in town while he was gone, and he wanted to get out of the Dodge pickup, which was terribly crowded with three people in the seat.

Shelby was anxious to see Chase, but he was

also apprehensive. After all, he didn't really believe that story about Brass himself. It was just too damned outlandish, too preposterous. It was an Indian version of a kid's fairy tale. No. He didn't believe it himself. Or did he? What else was there to believe? There had been a pole out in the ocean with two crows sitting on it. And they had acted mighty strange for crows— like they were guarding the pole.

And then there had been the alligator. Shelby had seen that with his own eyes. He had pulled up the pole, and it had been as if the alligator had been pulled up with it—a giant alligator out of his natural habitat with a monstrous scar on his belly. A scar where the pole had been run through to pin him to the bottom of the ocean? *No*, thought Shelby. *It can't be. It's too—Well, it's bullshit*. He parked the pickup almost in front of the police station and jerked open the door.

"Come on," he said. "Bring your book."

Jim Green, carrying his tattered copy of the 19th Annual Report of the Bureau of American Ethnology, came out the opposite door, followed immediately by Kay Shelby. Through the window in his office, the chief of police saw them enter the station. He ran to his office door, yanked it open, and yelled.

"Shelby, get in here."

Shelby, Kay, and Green hurried into the

chief's office, and Chase shut the door behind them.

"Hello, Miz Shelby," he said. He looked at Green. "Who's this?"

"This is Jim Green, Chief," said Shelby. "He's director of Native American Studies up at the university, and, uh, he's a Cherokee Indian."

Chase nodded cursorily at Green.

"Well, I want to talk to you in private, Shelby," he said.

"No, uh, I don't think so. I don't believe you do, Chief," Shelby said. "Why don't you listen to what we have to tell you first?"

Chase looked hard at Shelby, then Kay, then Green. He walked around behind his desk and sat down heavily, heaving a great sigh.

"All right," he said. "Let's have it."

"Chief," said Shelby, "you remember I told you an old Indian man warned me not to work on that beach? Said it was a bad place?"

"Yeah," said Chase.

"And then you remember the way those two crows acted anytime we got close to that pole?"

"Uh-huh."

"Then you know what happened when we pulled up the pole."

"Get to the point, Shelby."

"When I left here," Shelby said, "I went out to the reservation to find that old man. He said he didn't know anything more, except just the name of that place. He called it *kagunyi*. Said he didn't know what it means. It's not from his language. He said some people from another tribe came through here a long time ago and did something there and then named that place *kagunyi*. His grandson said he thought it was a Cherokee word and told us to go see Mr. Green here."

Green stepped up to Chase's desk and handed the chief the BAE Report opened to Wonder Tales, number 63.

"I showed them this," he said.

Chase looked up, his face wrinkled in incredulity.

"Wonder Tales?" he said.

"Read it, Chief," said Shelby. "Just read it."

Chase took out a cigarette and offered the pack around. Shelby and Green each took one. Kay declined. Then Chase settled back to read.

Shelby paced the floor. He smoked two of Chase's Marlboros before the chief had finished the story and closed the book.

"Well, Chief?" he said.

Chase pushed the book away from himself with the backs of his fingers, lit another cigarette, and leaned back in his chair.

"Pinned him to the ocean floor, did they?" he said.

"Yeah," said Shelby.

"With a long pole that stuck up out of the water."

"And two crows on top for guards," said Kay.

"To keep the beavers away," said Green, "but they didn't count on the U.S. Army Corps of Engineers."

Shelby felt the sting of Green's remark but decided to let it pass. After all, he thought, it was probably deserved.

"And he can take any shape he wants?" said Chase.

"That's what the story says," said Green.

"They call the place—what's that word?" asked the chief.

"*Kagunyi*," said Shelby.

"It means crow place," said Green.

Kay added, "And that's what the old man called it, too."

"The story says he can't die," said Chase.

"But he can be stopped," said Shelby. "He can be captured and pinned down again."

"Goddamn it," said the chief, pounding his desk and standing up behind it. "Goddamn it. It fits. It's insane, but it fits."

"Don't tell me that you're going to buy this story just like that," said Shelby.

The chief walked over to the window on the outside wall of his office and stared out into the street. He took a long drag on his cigarette.

"God, this was a quiet little town," he said.

"Ideal retirement community. All it needed was a nice, clean beach."

Shelby thought that Chase looked tired—tired and somehow older, even though it had been only a short time since he had last seen him. He wondered if the recent bizarre events had taken a similar toll on him. He certainly felt tired. Chase turned back at last to face the others in the room.

"A lot has happened here in a short time," he said. "A lot more even just since you left. I had three cops down there on the beach. Now, I didn't see any of this, but here's what I was told happened down there. One of the cops had his neck broken. It was done by a man. A naked man. Big. Long hair. Dark, we think, but it happened after sundown.

"The other one was killed by . . . a giant bird—hawklike. It gripped his head in one claw and carried him up in the air. Squeezed his head until it popped, then dropped him. I didn't see it happen, but there was a witness, and I saw the body. Saw both bodies."

"Oh, my God," said Kay.

"That sounds like *Tlanuwa*," said Green.

"*Tlanuwa?* What's that?" Shelby asked.

"*Tlanuwa* is a mythical, giant hawk from the old Cherokee tales," said Green. "You can find the story right there in Mooney. If the stories are based on reality—if Brass is real—then Brass would know *Tlanuwa*."

"That's not all," said Chase. "If it hadn't been for this next thing I'm going to tell you, I'd have all of you locked up by now for loonies. Including a couple of my cops. But I'm as loony as the rest of you. I saw this next myself.

"Two of my cops arrested a man for impersonating a police officer. He had on the uniform of the man whose neck had been broken on the beach—or at least, he had one just like it. The body was still dressed, so the guy had a copy, I guess.

"Anyhow, we brought him in here—right in here—for questioning. When they started to put the cuffs on him, he went nuts. He fought us. I was thrown right out through the door, into the squad room. When I looked back up—damn me to hell if I'm not telling the God's truth—there was a grizzly bear in here. Biggest damn bear I ever saw. He killed the two cops. The mayor crawled under the desk to hide, or he'd be dead now too."

"They mayor was here?" asked Shelby. "He saw all this?"

"Yeah," Chase said. "I sent a man for a rifle, but when he brought it back, and we came in here, there was no bear here. Just the bodies, the blood, and the mayor hiding under the desk. And I'd been right there outside that door the whole time. Watching. Where that bear came from or where he went, I'll never know."

"He could have changed to something very small and walked right out," said Green. "A bug, a fly."

The room was silent for a long moment. Then Jim Green stood up and walked over to the desk. He picked up his book and stared at it for a moment, almost as if looking at it for the first time.

"Chief," he said, "Mr. Shelby, Mrs. Shelby, I came down here out of intellectual curiosity, but now I'm afraid that the only thing we can do is assume that this old tale is genuine history—and that Brass is alive."

The door to the chief's office opened, and the policeman called Phil stuck his head in. He was holding a sheet of paper in his hand.

"Chief?" he said.

"What the hell is it, Phil?" said Chase. "I'm busy here."

"I think you'll want to see this," Phil said.

Phil walked on in and handed Chase the paper, then left again, closing the door behind himself. Chase read the report carefully, then dropped it on the desk in front of himself.

"Well," he said, "there've been two more killings. Out on the coast highway north of here. They might not be related to these others, but they're strange enough to consider. The remains of a man were found down in the median. It looked like the buzzards had been at him, but the coroner's examination indicated that he had been stabbed by some long, thin instrument, like an ice pick, but longer. It had been run into the underside of his chin, through the brain, and out the top of his skull. The man's ID was still with the body. His name was Carl Stokes."

"That could be Spearfinger's work," said Green.

"What?" said Chase.

"Spearfinger's another character from Cherokee mythology," Green said. "If these stories are really true, and if we're really dealing here with Brass, she's another character he would know and could imitate. She has a long finger, like a spear, or an awl. She's sometimes called Awlfinger."

"Shit," said Shelby.

"In the old tale," Green said, "Spearfinger looked like someone's grandmother. You know, a sweet little old lady. She'd entice kids to come and sit on her lap, and then she'd poke her long finger through them and kill them and eat them. The Cherokees dug a pit and trapped her and killed her. But like I said, if the stories are true, then Brass would surely know about her."

"Ugh," said Kay. "She was a cannibal?"

"Yeah," said Green. "Well, maybe. Of course,

she wasn't really quite human, now was she? Like Brass."

"Something had been eating on Stokes," Shelby said. "You don't suppose . . ."

"Could be," Green said.

"Ugh," said Kay again. "This gets worse all the time."

"Anyhow," said Chase, "it looks like Stokes was killed and his car was stolen. The car was found a few miles on down the highway in the parking lot of a roadside café, and that's where the second body was found.

"This one died from two bites from a brown recluse spider, the report says. Judging from the amount of poison in his system, a very large one. There was no identification on this body, no money except pocket change. The waitress in the café remembers that he paid for his meal with folding money from a hip pocket wallet, so it looks like he was robbed. The robber probably took his money, his car keys, and his car and left Stokes's car there."

"Would Brass be stealing cars and money?" Kay asked.

"Would a spider?" said Shelby.

"If he's taken on the form of a modern man," said Green, "he could have picked up an accomplice somehow—someone who knows how to drive and knows about money."

"All right. Just hold everything," said Chase.

"I don't know a damn thing about Indians, mythology, Indian mythology or none of that shit, but this Brass thing is the only thing that makes any sense here, so we're going to investigate it, but we'll do it the only way I know how. First off, I've got a few questions. Just how old are these damn stories?"

"Hundreds, maybe thousands of years," said Green, "but they weren't written down in this form until somewhere between 1887 and 1890."

"Then the characters in these stories are talking Cherokee. Right?" said Chase. "And Brass was pinned down to the ocean floor before Columbus came along, and even Columbus didn't talk English. If Brass never heard a word of English, and if this is Brass we're dealing with, how come he can talk English?"

"I can only guess," said Green. "In the old stories, everyone can talk to each other. It doesn't seem to matter what tribe they come from or what their language is. Even animals talk to each other and to people. Plants too.

"And remember that Brass isn't human. In his proper form, if we can call it that, he is like a human, like an Indian, but he's superhuman, a kind of spirit human, I guess. Maybe Brass can talk to anyone. Maybe he has a gift of communication of some kind where he just automatically understands any language he encounters. You know, in that old story, Brass lives a long ways off from the Cherokees, yet when the Cherokee boy comes by his house, they talk to each other."

"That sounds pretty far-fetched," said Shelby.

"Doesn't all of it?" answered Green.

"Okay," said Chase, "I'll buy it. For now. Now, what else do we know about this suspect? We know that we could walk right up to him and not realize it. We know that. He could be that goddamned fly buzzing in here right now, for all we know. What else do we know about him?"

"Well, according to the story, he had a wife," said Kay.

Chase had already begun taking notes, and he continued to scrawl hastily on the notepad before him.

"All right," he said. "Good. So he likes women."

"His main passion is gambling," said Green.

"And we think he's heading north," said Shelby, "and he might have someone with him."

"Oh," said Kay, "God help whoever that might be."

Again they fell into a silence. Chase made a last note on his pad, then took out a cigarette. He offered the pack, but the others all declined. He lit his own and drew deeply.

"So he's headed north," he said. "Probably with an accomplice. And he's probably looking for women and gambling. If we can get an ID on that brown recluse victim, we'll know what kind of car to look for. If they haven't switched again by then."

"So what do we do now?" said Kay.

"I'm going after him," said Shelby. "I've got to. I'm the one that turned him loose on the world. I've got to try to stop him. You can't do it, Chase. It's out of your jurisdiction."

"Who's going to tell me I can't pursue a mythological monster anywhere I want to?" said Chase. "And who's going to know? We can't tell this shit to anyone else. We'll both go."

"Well, I'm going with you," said Kay, "and don't even try to stop me."

"Me too," said Green.

Shelby turned to face Green.

"Look here," he said. "I only went to you for information. That's all, and you've been a big help in that area, but this thing could get us all killed. You don't have to come along on this. You don't need to go."

"Yes, I do," said Green.

"Why?" said Shelby. "How come?"

"My name," said Green.

"What?"

"My Indian name is *Anagalisgi*."

"Yeah? So what? What's that mean?"

"Lightning," said Green. "It means Lightning."

Chapter Thirteen

Judith Ann was tired. She had sneaked out of her house, walked to the highway, been picked up and attacked by Leon, met Brass, driven Carl Stokes's car to the café, watched while Brass had killed Leon somehow, robbed the body, stolen Leon's car, and driven most of the rest of the night away.

"Hey, man," she said, "let's stop at a motel. What do you say? We've got plenty of money now. Leon must have had three or four hundred bucks on him."

The motel was a pretty damn good idea, she

thought. Not only was she too tired to keep driving, but she felt too vulnerable, too visible driving the big T-bird in the broad daylight. She figured they could hide out in motel rooms during the day and drive at night. She'd feel a little safer that way.

"I don't understand," said Brass. "I don't know those things: motel . . . bucks."

"Oh, shit, man," said Judith Ann. "I swear to God you're going to drive me crazy. You know, it's a good thing I like you."

Brass wondered if Judith Ann would still like him if she should see him in his proper shape. For now, he was glad that he had chosen a shape that appealed to her, and he decided that he would keep it, at least for a while. Perhaps someday he would be able to tell her the truth about himself. Perhaps, but for now he wouldn't worry about it, and he wouldn't worry her with it.

"I like you too, Judith Ann," he said.

"Say," she said. "You got another name?"

"My name is Brass," he said.

"Just Brass?" she said.

"Yes," he said. "Just Brass. That's my name."

"Well, Just Brass," she said, "if we stop at a motel, you'll have to have another name, you know? You can't go around with just one name."

"I have to have two names?" he asked.

"Yeah, man," she said. "Like, my name's Judith Ann Baylor. See?"

"That's three names," he said.

"Okay," she said. "So, two or three, but not just one."

"I don't have another one," he said.

"Everyone has more than just one name," she said.

"I don't have."

"Well, then," said Judith Ann, "we'll just make one up. How about John? We'll call you John Brass. Okay?"

"Okay," he said.

"Now, then," she said, "bucks is money. You got that? Money is what you need to get anything. The more you got, the better. You need money to stop at a motel. A motel is a place to sleep. Now I'll start all over again. You want to stop at a motel?"

"Yes," he said. "That sounds good to me."

"We'll have to say that we're married," she said. "You know that?"

"No," said Brass, "but it's all right. I don't mind."

Judith Ann laughed.

"You know," she said, "it might be all right at that."

"Chase," said Shelby, "I think I ought to call Washington. I think we're about to go off half-cocked here. Can I use your phone?"

"Wait a minute," said Chase. "What the hell for?"

"Well, in the first place," Shelby said, "we're all liable to lose our jobs if we just take off without letting anyone know what the hell we're up to. In the second place, what if Brass wins? What then? We got to think about that possibility, you know. What if he kills us all? Somebody else has got to know what's going on, just what the hell the world has to deal with here. Does Brower know what's been going on here?"

"I can't be sure," said Chase, "but my best guess is that he does. He's been over at the mayor's office all day now. Whether or not he believes any of it is another question."

"Let's get him over here," Shelby said, "and find out just how much he does know and how much of it he believes. Maybe, if we can get him on our side, maybe between the two of us, me and the congressman, maybe we can convince General Niles of the truth of all this. If we get Niles's support, hell, that's like saying we got the whole damn government behind us."

"That makes sense to me," said Green. "I'm for it."

"Me too," said Kay.

"Right," said Chase. "I'll send somebody after Brower while you get Washington on the phone. The sooner we get organized and moving, the better. But just be careful who you say what to, Shelby. You hear?"

"Mr. and Mrs. John Brass," said Judith Ann, stepping into the center of the motel room. "I kind of like it."

Brass stood in the doorway, looking the room over.

"So this is motel," he said.

"Yeah," she said. "This is motel. Come on in."

She pulled him into the room, moved the Do Not Disturb sign from the inside doorknob to the outside one, shut the door, and hooked the chain lock.

"You want to watch TV?" she asked.

"I don't know," said Brass. "I don't know what TV is."

"Hell, I might have known," she said. "At least this will be easy. I'll just turn it on. That's all. Then you'll just see what it is."

Judith Ann turned on the television set. A news program was on. Brass's eyes opened wide in astonishment. He walked up close to the set, hesitated, then touched the screen. He was surprised to find it flat and smooth.

"Little people are in there," he said.

Judith Ann fell back on the bed, laughing.

"No, they're not," she said. "Those are just pictures. Moving, talking pictures. The real people are somewhere else."

"Pictures that move and talk?" Brass said.

"If you don't like what's on, you can change the channel," said Judith Ann. She sprang up from the bed, went back to the television set, and turned the channel selector knob. "Like this. There's all kinds of shit to watch on this thing. See?"

Brass moved in close to the set to watch carefully what she was doing.

"See?" she said. "You try it."

Brass reached out tentatively and turned the knob. He turned it again. He kept turning it while Judith Ann went back to the bed.

"Oh, God, I'm tired," she said. She looked at Brass, sitting there on the floor in front of the television set, still turning the knob, fascinated. *Where the hell did this guy come from, anyway?* she wondered. *Who the fuck is he? Brass. Just Brass. He's so fucking naive. So like a little kid. But not really like a retard. Not really. No. I don't think he's retarded.*

But he's a real man. That's for sure. He'll do anything. Just any damn thing. I wish I knew just how in hell he killed Leon. God. He did that just for me, too. Just for me. She realized that she had been inadvertantly massaging her breasts as she stared at the back of Brass's neck. She wanted him.

"Brass," she said.

Brass didn't answer. He was totally involved

with the channel-selector knob on the television set.

"Brass," she repeated, a little more loudly.

"Yes?" he said without looking away from the television screen. "What is it?"

"Do you think," she said, "that you could pick one channel and leave it there for a while?"

"Oh, sure," he said. "I'm sorry."

"It's okay," she said.

He found a Coca-Cola commercial and left it there.

"Come over here," said Judith Ann. She patted the mattress beside her. Brass stood up and walked over to the bed. Judith Ann was just lying there, looking up at him. She stretched out her left arm on top of the vacant pillow that was there beside her.

"Come on," she said.

Brass stretched himself out on the bed beside her, his head on the pillow, her arm under his neck. She pulled him to her, positioning his head on her breast. His left hand found her bare skin under the shirt and groped upward. Judith Ann twisted her face to find his lips with hers. She kissed him deeply, passionately, as his hand found her braless breasts. She broke away from the kiss, gasping for breath.

"It's okay," she said. "It's okay. I'm still a virgin, but it's okay. I'm Mrs. John Brass, right? You can fuck me. I want you to."

Brass crushed one breast in his hand and mashed his face against hers again. Judith Ann sucked hungrily at his mouth, then pulled away again.

"Come on," she said. "Let's get undressed."

They stood up on opposite sides of the bed from each other. Judith Ann slowly unbuttoned her shirt, then let it slide off her back and drop onto the floor. She smiled as Brass pulled off his shirt. Then she saw the ghastly scar on his belly.

"Oh God," she said. "What happened to you?"

"What?" said Brass.

"That awful scar," she said. "How did you get it?"

Brass looked down at his belly. He put both hands on the scar and rubbed it slowly.

"They hurt me," he said. "A long time ago."

Judith Ann hurried out of the rest of her clothing, then crawled back onto the bed, anxious for Brass to do the same. When he at last stood there before her, naked and ready, she reached out for him greedily and pulled him to her.

"Come on," she said. "Come on. I'll make you feel good."

It didn't take long. General Niles thought at first that Shelby had lost his mind, but Congressman Brower convinced him that at least he should get right on out to the West Coast in person. The story did, of course, sound mad, the congressman had said, but they had several unimpeachable witnesses, not to mention the fact that several very strange things had happened which could not be readily explained in any other way.

The general and the congressman agreed between the two of them that nobody else should be let in on the incredible story—at least not yet. In a matter of a few hours, Niles was in Chase's office. They showed him all the police reports, brought in all the witnesses. He even read the BAE report. It was a hard sell, but in another few hours Niles was a convert. There was simply nothing else for him to believe.

"Gentlemen," he said, "Mrs. Shelby, we've got to do our damndest to keep this thing quiet. We've also got to put a stop to this—this menace. You've been thinking about it for some time now. What do you propose?"

"Well, General," said Chase, "we can't do a damn thing until we locate him. We don't know yet what we'll do about it when we do find him, but we've got to find him first. So the four of us propose to go out looking for him right now. That's all."

"Where will you look?" Niles asked. "He could be anywhere."

"We'll just follow his trail north," Chase continued. "I don't know what else we can do. I've got men at work trying to get a make on the vehicle we think they're driving. If we get that information, we'll be a little better off."

"I'll stay here in your office, Chief," said the general. "You keep me informed about your progress. I'll clear it for the three of you men to be away from your jobs. Don't worry about that. Anything you need, you let me know."

"Well," said Shelby, "we can't all drive around in my pickup, but I've got a Travelall down at the site with the equipment. We could take that."

"What about your crew, Mr. Shelby?" said Niles. "Are they still hanging around here?"

"Yeah," said Shelby. "Yeah. They haven't been cut loose yet. I didn't really think I had that authority, you know?"

"I think, then," said the general, "that it would be best if they went right on back to work like nothing was wrong here. Don't you?"

"Well," said Shelby, "I, uh, I don't really see any reason why they shouldn't. I guess. If we're right about this thing, the danger is somewhere else now. It ought to be safe enough here."

"Exactly," said Niles. "I'll take care of it."

"I'll talk to Mike Murphy first," Shelby said. "I'll put him in charge of the crew and tell him if he has any questions or problems to come up here and see you. That sound all right?"

"Just fine," said Niles.

"I'll gather up some weapons from the station here," said Chase, "although I don't know if they'll be of any use to us."

"They might be," said Green. "We can't kill him, but we can hurt him—I think."

"When are we leaving?" Kay asked.

Chase looked each of the others in the face as he took a Marlboro out of his pack. It was his last one. He crumpled the pack and tossed it at the wastebasket beside his desk. He missed, and it fell on the floor.

"First thing in the morning?" he said. "All right?"

Judith Ann and Brass showered together, Brass marveling at the way the water came out of the pipe in the wall. They dried themselves off and walked back into the main room. Judith Ann went to the window and peeked out through the blinds.

"The sun's going down," she said. "We ought to get dressed and get out of here."

"Where will we go?" asked Brass.

"I don't know," she said. "Where do you want to go?"

"I don't know any place anymore," he said. "I don't know where to go."

Judith Ann wondered again about where Brass had come from. She wondered if he might have been in prison or something like that for a long time, but then, she didn't think that would really explain all of his peculiarities, the things that he just didn't know about.

"Well, what do you want to do?" Judith Ann asked him. "What do you like?"

"I like gambling," he said with a broad smile. "Do people still do that?"

"You sure are a funny one," she said with a little laugh. "Sure, people still gamble."

"Where do they gamble?" he asked.

"Hell," she said, "I don't know. I—yeah. Yeah, I do. Vegas. That's where."

"Vegas?" Brass said.

"Yeah. Vegas," she said. "Las Vegas, Nevada."

"Can we go there?" he asked, his voice and facial expression eager with sudden anticipation. "That's where I want to go—to Vegas to gamble."

"I don't really know how to get there," Judith Ann said, "but I guess we can get us a map. Yeah. We'll get a map, and we'll find it. Hell, yes, we can go to Vegas. Look out, Vegas, here we come."

Chapter Fourteen

Driving across the state line into Nevada, Judith Ann discovered one of the drawbacks of night driving, as well as a drawback to the large Thunderbird engine. The car was dangerously close to running out of gasoline, and she didn't relish the thought of having to abandon the luxurious automobile for a long walk in the cool desert air. She was on the verge of giving up hope when she saw a sign indicating a small town just two miles ahead. She drove the two miles, then took the exit into the town. The whole town was dark. She found a gas station and pulled in, but it was closed.

"Damn it," she said. "We'll have to stay here until morning when they open up again."

"We can't get gas here?" Brass asked.

"It's closed," said Judith Ann. "The god-damned station is closed. It won't open up again until sometime in the morning. Shit."

"The car won't go anymore?" Brass asked.

"Not very far," she said. "If we run out of gas out on the highway, we're stuck. Oh well, I saw a little motel back there. Let's go get us a room. It's better than sitting here for the rest of the night."

"Okay," said Brass, and he smiled happily at the prospects of "motel."

Judith Ann started to pull back out of the station's driveway, but just before she got the T-bird back into the street, she hit the brakes.

"Wait," she said.

"What is it?" he asked.

"I see a Coke machine," she said. "You want a Coke?"

Brass opened his lips as if to speak, and Judith Ann anticipated his response. She clapped a hand over his mouth.

"Don't say it," she said. "I'll just get you one, and we'll see if you like it."

She backed the car up to the machine and got

out. Brass watched carefully as she dropped the coins into the slot, then pushed a button. He heard the thump of the falling can and saw her reach down to get it. She handed it to him through the window.

"It's cold," he said.

"It better be," said Judith Ann.

He watched again as she repeated the procedure, then got back into the car with the second can of Coke.

"Look here," she said.

She hooked a thumbnail under the tab on top of the can and popped it back. Brass imitated her movements. She took a swallow from her can, and he took one from his.

"You like it?" she asked.

"It's good," he said. "But it's cold."

They had to wake up the night clerk to get a room at the little motel, but that done, they soon settled in for the rest of the night. Judith Ann was annoyed at first that her plans for driving at night and lying low in the daylight had been upset, but she soon got over that. The room had no television set, so they drank their Cokes, undressed, and crawled into bed. Judith Ann was still a little sore from the last time, yet she wanted him again. She pulled him over on top of her and spread her legs, allowing him to slip in between them.

"Fuck me," she said.

"Yes. Fuck," said Brass.

Shelby pulled the Travelall into the parking lot of the roadside café, and everyone climbed out.

"This is the place where the body was found," said Chase. "Right out here. His car keys were gone and so was his wallet. The Stokes car was abandoned close to the body. Right about there, I'd say."

"This was the spider-bite victim?" Kay asked.

"That's right," Chase said.

They went inside and sat down in a booth. It took a few minutes for a waitress to get around to them.

"Coffee all around," said Chase.

She left and came back a minute later with the coffee.

"Anything else?" she asked.

"Yeah," said Chase, flashing his badge. "Were you working the night the stiff was found out there?"

"No," she said, "but Myrna was. She waited on him."

"Is she here?" asked Chase.

"Yeah."

"Would you ask her to come over here for a minute, please?"

The waitress shrugged, chomped her gum, and walked away.

"Did that mean yes?" Green asked.

"It was hard to tell," Kay said.

Shelby slurped at the hot coffee in his cup.

"You think we can find out anything more here, Chief?" he asked. "I mean, the cops have already investigated this whole thing pretty thoroughly, haven't they?"

Chase gestured futilely with his big, clumsy-looking hands.

"It's the last place we've got him located," he said. "We got to try."

A waitress walked warily up to the booth. She put her hands on her hips and cocked her head to one side.

"You want to see me?" she asked.

"Yeah," said Chase. "You Myrna?"

"Yeah," she said.

Chase flashed his badge once more.

"The other gal said you waited on the guy that died outside the other night from the spider bites," he said. "Is that right?"

"Yeah," she said.

"You know the guy?"

"I seen him before," she said, "but I didn't know him. He stopped here sometimes. I think he was some kind of traveling salesman or something."

"You know his name?" Chase asked.

"Never heard it," she said. "Never asked, either."

"He use credit cards?"

"Cash," she said. "Always cash. We don't take credit cards here, or checks neither. He always asked for receipts, too."

"Was he a big spender?"

"Always the same thing. Hamburgers and apple pie," she said. "Apple pie with cheese. You ever hear of apple pie with cheese? Yuck. Black coffee. Lousy tips. He was a real tightwad."

"What makes you say that?" Chase asked.

"Like I said. Lousy tips," said Myrna. "And I seen the wad he carried in that billfold, too. He had plenty, believe me. I seen it. More than once. And that big car, too."

Chase perked up. Here was some new information.

"What kind of car?" he asked.

"A big T-bird," she said. "New one. Late model, anyhow."

"You notice the tags?" he asked.

"Nah," she said. "You think I got time to study car tags? Even if I had the time, why would I care?"

"Shit," said Chase, almost under his breath. He knew that had been too much to hope for anyway. "Was anybody with him that night? He talk to anybody? You see anyone watching him, or anyone follow him outside?"

"No," said Myrna. "I didn't see nothing like that. He come in here, ate his hamburger and apple pie—with cheese—drank a couple cups of coffee, paid for it, and left. That's all. Say, why all these questions, anyway? He was bit by a spider, right?"

"Right," said Chase, "but the body was robbed, and we don't know who the victim was. We're trying to get an identification on the body."

"Oh," she said. "Well, I don't know who the hell the guy was. Don't care, neither."

Brass got up from the bed and stretched. He went into the bathroom and washed himself, then went back out and pulled on his trousers.

"You want another . . . Coke?" he said.

"No," said Judith Ann. "I don't. Not right now."

"Well, I do," he said. "Show me which money to use."

Judith Ann found the change and handed him the right amount.

"Can you do it?" she asked.

"Yes," he said. "I watched you."

"Hurry back," she said as he left the room.

Brass walked back to the service station. He enjoyed the cool night air and the feel of the earth under his bare feet. He found the machine and dropped the coins in, then pushed a button. Nothing happened. He pushed the button again. Still nothing. He pushed it several times, hard and fast, and then he bashed it with his fist. Still he had no Coke. He braced himself firmly on both feet, squarely before the stubborn, cheating machine, and grasped it firmly in both hands. He began to shake it and to growl, and as he did he was overcome by his own real and proper shape. It was Brass, *Untsaiyi*, the ages-old monster, confronting the Coca-Cola machine, symbol of the modern age. His growl became a ferocious roar.

Behind the station the door to a mobile home was thrown open from the inside, and a stubby, slavering pit bull rushed forth, ready and eager for combat. Brass was so intent on the offensive Coke machine that he was unaware of the chunky brute until it had fastened its sharp teeth deep in the flesh of his right calf, biting even through the hard inner shell of brass and causing the blood to run freely down his leg.

He screamed and whirled to face his surprise attacker, the force of his spin flinging the dog through the air and causing its teeth to rip on through the muscle on his leg. The little monster snarled and rushed at him a second time. Brass kicked ferociously, catching the beast in the jaw. It flinched and stalled, losing a couple of seconds in its attack.

Back at the mobile home a light had come on, and a man stood in the open doorway.

"Get him, Waldo," he yelled. "Get the god-damned son of a bitch."

Across the street, the front door of a small frame house opened, and a middle-aged woman in a nightgown stepped out on the porch.

"I'm calling the cops," she shouted in a shrill voice. "I warned you about that killer dog."

She disappeared back in the house and slammed the door behind her.

The pit bull, having recovered from the kick to its jaw, bunched itself for another lunge but paused again, this time in astonishment. He found himself facing, not a man, but another pit bull, almost identical to himself. The new arrival stood squarely on all fours, a low rumble coming from deep down in his throat. His teeth were bared and dripping saliva.

Then, almost as if at a prearranged signal, the two mini-monsters rushed each other. They bounced back slightly at the impact of their two bodies meeting with such force. Then the new one made a quick pass and grasped the other's ear between his teeth. He whipped his head back and forth, ripping the ear away from the head. Seemingly oblivious to pain and injury, Waldo leapt madly at his adversary, wrapping his short forelegs around the other's head, trying for a bite on the spine.

* * *

A siren cut through the night air, and a police car screeched to a halt in the gas station driveway. Two doors flew open and a policeman came out of each one, each with a gun in his hand. The two dogs were spinning, snarling, flinging blood around on the cement.

"Goddamn," said one of the cops. "What do we do, Jeff?"

"Shoot the damn things," Jeff answered.

"Both of them?"

"Damn it," said Jeff. "Just shoot."

The dogs bashed into a steel trash can that stood beside the Coke machine just as the cops started firing. The can fell over and rolled out clattering into the driveway, spilling oil cans, used rags, and other trash in its wake. There was some brief yelping, then an eerie silence. The two police officers looked at each other, then walked slowly over toward the machine to inspect the results of their handiwork.

"Hey, Jeff."

"What?" said Jeff.

"There's only one dead dog here," said the other.

"Well, where the hell's that other one?" Jeff asked.

"I don't see it anywhere."

"He can't have just disappeared," Jeff said.

"We got to find that son of a bitch. He's dangerous."

From behind the Coke machine, a small gray mouse watched as the two nervous policemen set out on a search for the missing dog.

Chapter Fifteen

He had been amazed at the buildings and
streets of a small city in the daylight hours. The
noises and the crowds of people and their
strange behavior had astonished him. He had
been both perplexed and intrigued by the trans-
portation machines, which he now knew were
called cars, but which he had first believed to
be giant, domesticated bugs. He had marveled
at his first glimpse of electric lights in use and
at television, but he remained totally unpre-
pared for the shocking sight of his first entry at
night into the city of Las Vegas, Nevada.

Judith Ann was driving, even though he had learned to drive while on the trip. It had been a long ride to Las Vegas for Judith Ann, and she had welcomed the opportunity to teach him, but he had learned to drive out on the open highway, and he was still frightened by the confusion of city traffic.

It was early morning and still dark when Brass and Judith Ann drove into Las Vegas on Interstate Highway 15, and Brass was overwhelmed by the lights. Lights in all colors, flashing lights, lights in different shapes, lights down low at eye level, and lights up high in the sky on tall buildings and on posts. Brass couldn't read the signs, of course, so he didn't recognize the famous names of nightclubs, casinos, and hotels. He wouldn't have known the names had he been able to read them. Nonetheless, he gazed in wonder at the colorful, flashing spectacle of it all.

"It's the middle of the night," he said.

"Yeah," said Judith Ann with a yawn. The astonishment in brass's voice was lost on her.

"But it's like daytime here," he said.

"It's all the lights," she said.

"Not just lights," he said. "People. Look at all the people going in and out."

"Yeah," she said.

Judith Ann drove on into the heart of the city. It wasn't easy, but she found a space and parked the T-bird. She was relieved to get out of the car. She hadn't said anything to Brass, didn't want to worry him needlessly, but she had become increasingly afraid that the police might have discovered the identity of the body she and Brass had left behind in the café parking lot and might, even now, be searching for the stolen car. She left it, but she kept the keys.

"Where's the gambling?" asked Brass, turning around and looking at the tall buildings and the lights, his eyes wide with wonder.

"I think it's just about everywhere," said Judith Ann, "but we've got to find a hotel first and get us a room."

"Okay," he said, "but hurry." He was still looking all around, and he was itching to gamble. It had been an eternity, and now he was used to being free again. He'd had good meals, and he had a woman. That had all been enough for a while, but now he was ready to play.

"Over there," said Judith Ann, pointing across the street. "There's one. Come on."

Brass followed Judith Ann, dodging cars to cross the street, to the hotel she'd selected. At the desk, once again she registered for them both as Mr. and Mrs. John Brass.

"We'll bring our luggage in later," she told the desk clerk, taking the key to the room. As she turned away from the desk, she spotted the slot machines in the hotel lobby.

183

"Look," she said.

"What is it?" Brass asked.

Judith Ann noticed the signs prohibiting the use of slot machines by minors. She would have to tell Brass what to do and keep her distance.

"It's gambling machines," she said. "They're like the Coke machine. Remember?"

Brass remembered the Coke machine well, but the powerful urge to gamble overcame the bad memory.

"You put your money in the slot," she said, "and pull the handle down. See the pictures?"

"Yes," he said.

"After you pull the handle," she continued, "the pictures turn. When they stop, if they're all the same, you win. Here. Try one."

She handed him a quarter and watched from a respectful distance. Brass stepped over to the machine she had designated. He looked at it, saw the slot, and dropped in the quarter. He pulled the handle and the pictures spun. His heart raced with the spinning pictures. They stopped suddenly, and quarters started pouring into the tray at the bottom of the machine.

"I won," he shouted. "Judith Ann, look. I won. I won. Ha, ha!"

Judith Ann, too, jumped up and down with excitement, joining him in his ecstasy. She laughed and clapped her hands.

"I'll play some more," he said, reaching for

one of the quarters piled in the tray.

"No," said Judith Ann. "Not yet. Not the same machine."

"Why not?" he asked.

"That machine won't pay off again," she said. "Not for a while. Get the money, and let's go to the room."

Shelby pulled the Travelall onto the shoulder, even though signs indicated that the shoulders were for emergency parking only. Up ahead was a directional sign informing motorists of an exit ramp just ahead for Interstate Highway 15 going east to Barstow and on to Las Vegas, Nevada. Shelby sat and stared at the sign.

"Well, what do you think, gang?" he said.

"Las Vegas, of course," said Kay. "He is the Gambler."

"I'd make a bet on it," said Green.

"Let's go for it," said Chase.

Shelby looked over his shoulder to find a break in the oncoming traffic, then goosed the Travelall and headed it for the ramp.

"Vegas it is," he said.

Brass got out of the bed and began picking up his clothes from the floor. His motions brought Judith Ann, naked on top of the sheets, out of her sleep. She rubbed her eyes with the back of her hand.

"Where are you going?" she asked.

"To play," he said. "I've got lots of money."

"Brass," she said, "sit down."

He pulled on his trousers and sat on the edge of the bed.

"I've got to try to explain some things to you," she said.

"What things?" he asked.

"Well, money, to start with," she said. "We don't have lots of money. Those quarters you got, it takes four of them to make a dollar. And Don—that's my shit stepdad—he makes fifty thousand dollars a year, and he's always saying we ain't got enough money."

"Fifty thousand dollars?" said Brass.

"That's right," she said.

"Four quarters makes one dollar?"

"Yeah," she said, "and this here room is costing us plenty for just one night. Fifty bucks. It'll cost fifty more for each night we stay here. And we have to eat, and that costs money. It takes a lot of money to live in Vegas."

"Then I should go out and play," Brass said, "and win more money."

Judith Ann sighed heavily. Talking to Brass was sometimes like talking to a child, she thought. Sometimes? She corrected her own thought. Almost always.

"Let me tell you about Vegas," she said. "Don comes here sometimes, and I've listened to him talk to Mom about it. I seen a show about it, too, on TV."

"Okay," he said.

"These games are all rigged, you know? Take that slot machine you played. It probably pays off every so many times the handle gets pulled. You know what I mean?"

"Yes," he said. He was listening attentively and thoughtfully now. He was anxious to get back to the gambling, but he also liked to win, so if Judith Ann had information he needed, he would wait a little longer.

"You were just lucky you happened to be the one who came along when it was time for it to pay," she said. "That's all."

"Just luck, huh?" he said.

"That's right," she said.

"No," said Brass. "There's something more."

"What?" said Judith Ann. "What are you talking about?"

"If the games are . . . rigged," he said, "then somebody knows how they're rigged. I'll have to find out about that. I'm a good gambler. Back where I used to live, a long time ago, everyone called me that—the Gambler. So tell me more about Vegas."

Brass walked into the big casino. He had never before been under so vast a roof. He had never seen such action, such intensity. The first area he came to was taken up by rows and rows of slot machines. He didn't want to appear to be either ignorant or suspicious, so he walked directly to a quarter machine and lost his quarter. He walked down the aisle and stopped at another machine. He lost another quarter.

Judith Ann was right, he thought. He played a third machine and lost again. Any other time the losing would have frustrated Brass, probably to the point of anger, but Judith Ann had prepared him well for this experience. He had come into the place knowing what to expect and why. He knew that these losses had nothing to do with his skill as a gambler. He remained calm and walked around the end of the row of machines, preparing to venture down another aisle, but he found himself confronted by a giant slot machine. A man in blue wearing a badge stood beside it. Brass's heartbeat responded to the sight of the cop, but he managed to maintain his outward appearance of calm.

"Hello," he said.

"Hi," said the cop.

"Is this Big Bertha?" asked Brass.

Judith Ann had told him about Big Bertha, the monstrous slot machine that had been one of the major focal points of the television show she had watched on gambling in Las Vegas. It was a dollar machine, and recently it had paid off a sum of five million dollars. Judith Ann had told him that, according to the show, the machine was hooked up by wires to another machine—she had called it computer—in another room, and that the other machine controlled Big Bertha, decided when she would pay off. He stared at her in wonder.

"That's her," said the cop.

Brass took out a silver dollar and tried Big Bertha. She swallowed the big coin without giving a sign of discomfort. Brass smiled at the cop, gave a casual shrug, and walked away.

He was back in the doorway to the same large casino as before. Inside, Big Bertha awaited, but there were people everywhere, it seemed. The world looks much different from the viewpoint of a cockroach. Everything is bigger, and feet—that is, the feet of human beings—become more threatening and ominous, especially when they are inside shoes with such hard, slick soles and are walking on very hard floors. He winced inwardly at the thought of being crunched between those two hard surfaces.

The best path, he decided, would be the edge of the floor up against the wall. His journey would be farther that way, but the risk out on the open floor was simply too great. He gathered his courage, thought about the goal, and began the trip. A foot came dangerously close about halfway to the corner of the room, and he ran as hard as his six skinny legs would carry him. He made it safely to the corner and stopped. His cockroach heart pounding furiously, he rested in the corner and watched. No one seemed to be aware of his presence. He made a dash for Big Bertha.

The darkness between the wall and the backside of the big machine was comforting, so he just sat there and rested himself for several minutes. By then his eyes had become adjusted to the darkness, and he started to look around. He found several wires, but there was one much bigger around than any of the others, and it went into a hole in the wall. *That must be the one,* he thought.

He climbed the wall up to the hole, then peered inside. It was absolutely dark. He would have to climb onto the wire itself and walk it by feel until he came to the end of the line. He clambered onto the wire and felt the shape of its mass beneath him. Then he inched his way into the total darkness beyond.

Kay closed the door behind her, checked to see that it was locked, and glanced at the word stenciled on the door. She thought that it would have been appropriate had it said "Women." "Ladies" seemed an awfully elegant label for the decor of the room she had just made use of. She walked back around to the front of the building and inside the office to return the key. Her husband was paying for the gasoline with his government credit card.

"You ready to go, babe?" he said.

"Yes," she said.

They got back into the Travelall, where Chase and Green were waiting. Shelby started the engine.

"I think we're on the right track," he said. "That guy in the station? He owns the joint. Lives in that trailer out back. He had a pit bull that he turned loose on what he thought was a prowler. The neighbor lady called the cops. When they showed up, there were two pit bulls fighting each other. The cops shot them, or they thought they did. When they quit shooting, they found one dead dog. His. The other one hasn't been seen since."

"You think it was Brass?" Chase asked.

"Could be," said Shelby. "The guy filled up a T-bird the same day. Man and woman in it, he said. They paid with cash. He thinks it had California tags."

"We don't know," said Chase, "that the T-bird we're looking for was licensed in California."

"No, hell," said Shelby. "I know that. We don't know that Brass killed the man or took the T-bird either. We don't know that he's got a woman with him. Hell, we don't know shit."

"Wait a minute," said Green. "Just for kicks,

let's assume that it was the same T-bird, and that Brass was the missing pit bull. What time of day did these things happen?"

"Well, I—Just a minute," said Shelby. He rolled down the window, shut off the engine, and called out to the station owner, who was standing in the doorway to his office. "Hey, buddy."

The station owner squinted. "Yeah?" he said.

"Could you come over here a minute?" Shelby asked.

The man strolled over to the Travelall, scratching through his coveralls at one side of his body.

"Yeah?" he said again.

"That T-bird you filled up," said Shelby, "what time of day was that?"

"I don't know," said the man. "It was morning. Kind of early."

"And the dog fight," said Shelby. "When did that happen?"

"Middle of the night, the night before. Why?"

"Okay, buddy," said Shelby. He started the engine again. "Thanks," he said, and he pulled the Travelall out onto the road. "Well?" he said.

"If both were Brass," said Green, "that means he was around here for a while."

"There's a motel right over there," said Kay.

"Let's check it," said Chase.

Shelby drove to the motel, and the four of

them got out and went inside the office. The clerk stood up behind the counter to greet them. Shelby flashed a federal ID card, and Chase showed his badge.

"We'd like to check your register," said Chase.

"Sure," said the clerk, properly intimidated.

He placed a file box on the counter and turned it toward Chase, who flipped a few cards, then pulled one out. He held it up for the others to see.

"You believe this?" he said.

"Mr. and Mrs. John Brass," read Kay.

"And," said Green, "they were driving a Thunderbird with California tags."

"That's bold," said Shelby. "Or stupid."

Chase laid the card on the desk facing the clerk.

"Do you remember these people?" he asked.

"Let me see," said the clerk. "Yeah. Well, that is, I remember her. I didn't really see him. She signed the card and paid for the room."

"Cash?" Chase asked.

"Yeah. Cash."

Chase took a notepad from his pocket and wrote down the license number from the card. He looked around the office, found a pay phone on the far wall, and went over to it. He shoved a hand into his pants pocket and pulled out his change. He scowled as he pushed the coins in his palm around with a finger of his other hand.

"Hey, Green," he called.

"Yeah?" Green said.

"You got a quarter?"

Green found one in his pocket and gave it to Chase, who then dialed his number while Shelby continued to question the clerk.

"You never saw the man?" Shelby was asking.

"No," said the clerk. "I don't think I ever did. Just when they first drove up. I could see that there was a man out there in the car, but that's all."

"What about the woman?" Shelby asked.

"Woman?" said the clerk with a little laugh. "I'd hardly call her that. Just a girl. No more than sixteen or seventeen, I'd say."

"Oh, no," said Kay.

"Did you find anything in the room after they left?" said Green.

"Three Co'Cola cans," said the clerk. "That's all."

Chase came back to the counter.

"I've got a trace on that license tag number," he said. "Let's go to Vegas."

The blackness reminded him of the worst times at the bottom of the ocean, the times when no light broke through the waters to give evidence of another world. He was conscious of climbing straight up for a while, then making a turn, and another turn, then losing all sense of direction. He clung tenaciously to the wire with his tiny feet and moved ahead in the void.

Chapter Sixteen

Brass came rushing into the hotel room so quickly that he startled Judith Ann into jumping up from the bed, where she had been lounging and watching an episode of *The Newlywed Game*.

"Judith Ann," he said excitedly. "Judith Ann."

"What?" she said. "What the hell is it? Is someone after you?"

"No," he said. "Nothing like that. I figured it out."

"Figured out what?" she asked. "What are you talking about? You never tell me everything. So start at the beginning. What did you figure out?"

He sat down, bouncing on the edge of the bed beside her, and took hold of her by the shoulders. He looked straight into her eyes, a broad smile on his face, and his eyes seemed to sparkle. She thought again that he was much like a child in many ways.

"I know when Big Bertha is scheduled to pay off," he said. "I found out."

"What?" she said, and she looked at him with an expression of disbelief on her face.

"Yeah," he said. "I know. A million bucks, Judith Ann. It's going to pay a million bucks. Will that be enough money for us?"

"A million bucks," said Judith Ann, starting to bounce on the edge of the bed herself. "A million bucks. Hell, yes. We'll be fucking millionaires."

She sprang to her feet, pulling him up with her, and together they danced and hopped around the room in tiny circles, laughing and chanting.

"A million bucks," they sang together. "A million bucks."

At last she fell straight back onto the bed and lay there to catch her breath.

"Wait a minute," she said, sitting up and looking him in the face again. "How do you know?"

"The guys in the computer room said when it would happen," he told her. "All I have to do is get a pocketful of silver dollars and be there to put them in the slot at the right time."

"How the hell did you get in the computer room?" she asked, giving him a sideways look.

"Never mind about that now," said Brass. "But I did. I did it, and nobody saw me either, and I heard them, and I know, and I'm going to win a million bucks."

"Well, all right," Judith Ann said. "When's it going to happen?"

"It's tomorrow night," he said, "between ten and twelve."

"Oh man," said Judith Ann, falling back again on the bed. "None too soon. Oh, wow."

"What's wrong, Judith Ann?" he asked her. "Is something wrong?"

"These fucking hotel people have been bugging me today," she said. "They want their goddamned money, and we ain't got enough left here to pay the bill."

"I've got some money," said Brass. He emptied out his pockets, pouring a pile of loose change, including a few silver dollars, out onto the bed. "You can have it all," he said.

Judith Ann fingered the coins, making a quick count.

"That's still not enough," she said. "And even if it was, if we was to use it all to pay the hotel bill, what would you use tomorrow night for Big Bertha?"

Brass walked across the room, rubbing both his hands in his hair. He turned back to face Judith Ann, his face now a mask of worry and confusion.

"Well," he said, "what are we going to do?"

In another hotel room not far away, a phone rang, and Harvey Chase moved quickly to pick it up. The other three people in the room stopped talking and sat still in quiet anticipation.

"Yeah," said Chase. "This is Chase. Okay. Okay. Good. No. No, don't do anything about it. And thanks. Thanks a lot."

He hung up the receiver and turned to face the others in the room.

"The Vegas cops found the car," he said. "It's right here. Downtown collecting parking tickets at a meter right out here on the street."

"That probably means they've abandoned it," said Shelby.

"Probably," Chase agreed. "It also probably means that we were right, and they're somewhere here in Vegas. Come on. Let's go take a look at the car."

Judith Ann opened the door a crack and peered out into the hallway. She watched as a man in a short-sleeved shirt with a floral design walked by, stopped at another door, took a key out of his pocket, fumbled with the lock a moment, and then disappeared into a room.

"Come on," she said. "It's clear."

She led Brass out into the vacant hallway and walked quickly toward a lighted sign at the far end that read, "Exit." Close behind her, Brass carried a small leather suitcase packed with clothes they had purchased since their arrival in Las Vegas. Judith Ann opened the door beneath the exit sign.

"Come on," she said.

Behind the door they found a stairway, and they started down.

"Will they see us?" Brass asked.

"No," she said. "I don't think so. Come on. We got to get out of here."

At the bottom of the stairway were two doors, one marked "Lobby," the other, "Emergency Exit Only." Judith Ann looked over her shoulder, took a deep breath, shoved the handle, and opened the emergency exit, instantly setting off a loud and piercing alarm.

"Let's go," she said, and she ran out into the alley, Brass running alongside her. At the end of the alley, she ducked around a Dumpster and stopped. He stopped beside her, and they stood there, their backs pressed against the wall.

"Now," she said, "we catch our breath, and we walk out on the street, real calm and easy like. We act like nothing's wrong. Got it?"

"I got it," Brass said.

"Okay," said Judith Ann. She took his hand in hers, stuck her nose up in the air, and strolled out onto the sidewalk.

"What now?" Brass asked her.

"Smile," she said.

He did.

"But what are we going to do?" he said.

"Well," she said, "I guess we're just going to walk around awhile and find ourselves a cheaper hotel and check into a room there, and then tomorrow night you'll get rich on Big Bertha, and everything'll be all right. We'll have all the money we need. We might even go back and pay these creeps what we owe them. Who knows?"

They had reached the corner and stopped to wait for the light to change so they could cross the street. Brass glanced back down the sidewalk over his shoulder.

"Look," he said.

Judith Ann turned her head and saw three men and a woman about halfway down the block inspecting the abandoned Thunderbird. She jerked her head back to the front and watched the light. Her face flushed purple.

"Don't look at them," she said.

"Why not?" he asked.

The light changed, and she started to cross the street, pulling Brass behind her.

"Come on," she said. "Let's get the hell away from here."

"What's wrong?" he asked.

"It's cops," she said.

"They don't have blue clothes," he said.

"Some cops don't wear blue clothes," she said. "God, don't you know anything? They're called plainclothes cops."

"Then how do you know they're cops?" he asked.

"They just have to be," she said. "That's all. They traced that car, and they followed us here. They're looking for us."

Judith Ann spotted a hotel on the far corner of the block and across the street. It seemed a likely one, a bit sleezy perhaps, but then, she figured they didn't have much choice.

"We'll go there," she said, "but we'll have to change our names this time."

Shelby slapped the top of the T-bird with his open palm.

"Ah, hell," he said, "we didn't learn a damn thing here."

"Except that they've been here," said Kay. "We know that now for sure. Don't we?"

"We've learned more than you think," said Chase. "Let's go get a cold beer and talk it over."

Jim Green looked over his shoulder at a small café just two doors down the street.

"How's that place?" he asked.

Shelby shrugged. "It's all right with me," he said.

"Come on," said Chase.

They went inside the café, found themselves an empty booth, and soon they had been served. Chase took a long drink from a frosted mug, then pulled out his cigarettes and lit one. He tossed the pack and his lighter out into the center of the table.

"Help yourselves," he said.

Shelby took one and lit it.

"Well," he said, "just what the hell did we learn out there, Chase?"

Chase expelled a cloud of smoke and slouched back into the booth.

"Like your wife said, Shelby," he started, "they've been here. We're close. We know that. We also know the identity of the spider-bite victim from the registration in the car. I'll probably get a call from home confirming it, because I put a trace on the license number, but we already know it now. So we can be pretty sure that our hunch was right.

"Brass killed Leon Hardin and stole his car, with the help of a sidekick, who is probably a female, teenage runaway. From there they drove up here to Vegas, and they're probably still here. We can assume that because of the same thing that brought us here in the first

203

place. The guy's a compulsive gambler. Now that he's here, why would he leave? Since they seem to have abandoned the car, they're probably registered at a hotel within walking distance of us right now."

"We don't know what the hell they look like," said Shelby, "so where does that leave us?"

"It leaves us right where I said," Chase said. "Close."

"So what do we do now?" Kay asked.

"Well," said Chase, "they were dumb enough once to sign a register using the name of Brass. Maybe they're dumb enough to do it again. Who knows? The guy's some kind of primitive, and the gal's just a kid. So we get the local cops to check the hotels around here for that name. That's the next step."

He emptied his glass and glanced around the table.

"Everyone ready?" he asked. "Let's go."

Chapter Seventeen

It was ten o'clock when the little old lady walked into the casino. Ignoring everyone and everything around her, she headed straight to Big Bertha. A big man in an expensive, western-cut suit stood before the mammoth slot machine, feeding it silver dollars. The uniformed guard stood to one side. The old lady walked up and stood with nervous irritation close behind the cowboy. She watched as he gave away five more silver dollars, then she poked a bony finger into the small of his back. He flinched and looked over his shoulder, then looked down to find her.

"Why don't you give someone else a chance at her, sonny boy?" she said. "You're not doing any good anyway."

The guard stepped forward menacingly.

"Lady," he said sternly, "with these machines, it's first come, first served. It ain't ladies first. You wait your turn like everyone else and don't bother people, or I'll have to ask you to leave the premises."

"Ah, hell, pardner, it's all right," said the cowboy. "The lady said it straight. I'm just giving away my money anyhow."

The tall cowboy left Big Bertha for the further enticements that waited deeper in the interior of the gambling den, and the old lady, giving the guard a crooked and self-satisfied sneer, stepped up to the machine. It loomed over her tiny frame. For a moment she just stood there, as if spellbound at the feet of an awesome mechanical idol, and then she slowly, apprehensively, reached out to lay a hand on it.

No sooner had she touched its skin than she quickly withdrew her hand, almost as if she had inadvertently touched a hot stove. Then she seemed to shake herself out of a reverie and busy both her hands with the undoing of the clasp of her worn old handbag. At last she got it opened. She stuck a bony hand deep into the bag and withdrew a shiny silver dollar, then stretched her arm out to reach with the dollar for the waiting slot. Her reach was an inch short of the mark. She tried to stretch her arm farther, tried to reach the mark, but she couldn't make it. She turned toward the guard, trembling with sudden rage and frustration.

"I can't reach it," she said.

The guard shrugged. Clearly, he thought it served her right. "Sorry, lady," he said.

"I can't reach the slot," she said, raising her voice, "and it's not fair."

"Sorry," the guard said, and the look on his face was smug.

"Well?" she said. "What are you going to do about it, buster?"

"There ain't nothing I can do about it," said the guard. "I can't move the slot, and I sure ain't going to hold you up there."

"Well," she shouted, "find me something to stand on. Hurry up."

"I don't know what—"

"Get me a chair," she demanded.

The old lady was getting louder with each of her demands, and the guard at last began to get nervous. People were watching now. She was drawing attention from all around the room, and his job was at least partially to prevent these kinds of embarrassing scenes. He glanced up at one of the many television security cameras that constantly scanned the casino's interior, conscious that someone up there was watching over him, taking note of how he was handling this situation.

"Okay, lady," he said. "Okay. Just calm down. Take it easy. I'll get you a chair. Okay?"

He brought a chair from a nearby table and shoved it up close to Big Bertha, then grudgingly helped the old lady step up onto the chair seat. From her new height, she smiled back down on him benignly.

"Thank you," she said. "You're very kind."

She looked back at Big Bertha, and her eyes lit up. She reached out and dropped the dollar into the slot. Nothing happened. She shoved her hand back into the bag and brought out another dollar. Slowly, carefully, she dropped it in. Nothing.

"Well, lady," said the scowling guard, "you satisfied now?"

She glared down at him, standing there with his arms crossed over his chest, then reached down into her purse for another dollar.

"No," she said. "I'm not."

Chase put down the telephone in the hotel room and turned to Green and Shelby. Kay was in an adjoining room taking a nap.

"That was the Vegas cops," said Chase as he finished writing a note to himself. "They found them, all right. Right down the street from us. They really were dumb enough to do it again.

Mr. and Mrs. John Brass. You believe that? You want to go along?"

"Sure," said Green.

"You're damn right," said Shelby.

"This could be dangerous," said Chase. "If Brass is there—well, you know what he can do."

"We've known about the dangers from the beginning," said Shelby.

"We're going," said Green.

"Okay," said Chase. "We'll take along some weapons on this trip."

Shelby opened the door to the adjoining room.

"You asleep, babe?" he said.

Kay raised herself up on one elbow and looked at him standing there in the doorway.

"No," she said. "What's going on?"

"We're going down the street to check a hotel," he said. "Looks like they're registered over there. You stay here till we get back. Okay?"

"Oh, God," said Kay.

"We're taking some guns," said Shelby, "just in case, but don't worry. We're not going in there like hot shots. We're just going to check it out."

"Be careful," she said. "Be real careful."

"We will," he said. "Promise."

He shut the door, and Chase handed him a revolver.

"A .44 Magnum," he said.

The three men, all armed, stepped out into the hallway. The other two waited while Shelby closed the door to their suite behind him and tested it to make sure it was locked. They looked at each other, then turned to walk down the hall toward the elevators, side by side and in step.

The three men, of course, had no way of knowing, as they left on their potentially dangerous mission, that just two doors down the hallway from the door to their own suite, they walked past the very room in which Judith Ann Baylor sat nervously watching an episode of *Dallas* on the television and alternately wringing her hands and biting her nails.

"They're gone now," said the desk clerk. "You're too late."

"Shit," said Shelby.

"When did they check out?" asked Chase.

"They didn't," the clerk said. "The shits sneaked out without paying their bill. If you find them, I hope you'll let us know."

"When did you find out they were gone?" asked Chase.

"Just this morning," the clerk answered. "They didn't answer the phone in the room, so we went up to check on them. Sure enough, they were gone. No one there. No clothes in the room. Nothing. They did leave both keys in there, thank God."

"What can you tell us about them?" said Chase. "Anything. Appearance. Anything at all."

"Why, nothing, I'm afraid," said the clerk. "Frankly, I don't remember them from when they checked in, and I don't recall ever seeing them to know who they were. We have a great many people come through here. I talked to her on the phone trying to get her to pay the bill. That's about it. Sorry."

"When was the last time you knew for sure they were still up there?" Chase asked.

"Yesterday afternoon, I'd say," said the clerk. "She answered that call. You know, I bet they left right after that. An alarm went off indicating that someone had opened an emergency door. I bet that was them bugging out on us."

"Did someone check that exit?" Chase asked.

"Oh sure," said the clerk, "but they were long gone. Whoever it was."

"Can we take a look at the room?" said Chase.

The clerk found a key and tossed it to Chase.

"Help yourself," he said, "but you won't find anything."

As they approached the room, the hotel maids were just going in. Chase broke into a run.

"Hold it," he yelled. "Don't go in there."

The two maids stopped and looked at Chase with stupid expressions on their faces. Shelby and Green ran up behind Chase, who was showing his badge to the maids.

"If you're just now getting around to this room," Chase said, "does that mean that it hasn't been cleaned since the people left here this morning?"

The maids looked at each other.

"Yeah," said one.

"Great," said Chase. "Well, I'm going to ask you to hold off on it for a while longer. Okay? We have to check it out."

"The manager told us to get up here and clean it," said one of the maids. "It didn't get cleaned earlier because the sign was out. You know, Do Not Disturb? We thought they were in there."

"Well," said Chase, "you just tell your manager that it'll have to wait a little longer. Okay? You tell him I said so. I've already talked to the guy down at the front desk, so it's all right. I'll let you know when we're done with it."

As the two maids shuffled off down the hallway pushing their cart, Chase turned to Shelby and Green.

"Come on," he said, "but don't touch anything."

They stepped into the room and looked around. The bed was unmade, but nothing seemed to have been left behind except a few empty Coca-Cola cans. Walking carefully, Chase looked into the bathroom. Towels and wash rags had been used and tossed onto the floor. He noticed that the water glasses had been unwrapped and used. So had the soap. He turned back to the others.

"There's nothing we can do here," he said, "but I'll call the Vegas cops back and have them send a lab crew over here. We might be able to get an ID on the girl from prints. If we're lucky. Let's go."

She had only two silver dollars left, and she had no idea what time it was getting to be. She could sense a panic building deep inside her guts. Suppose she should use her last dollar, and there were still just a few minutes left. Then suppose someone else came along and dropped in a dollar and won. After all that planning.

She shifted her feet on the chair like a batter searching for just the right stance before the pitch is thrown. She reached out and gently touched the machine that had become the center of her world. She stroked it. She glanced down at the guard and read on his face a look of impatience. Then she shoved her hand into the bag and withdrew a dollar for her penultimate play.

She inserted the coin halfway into the slot and held on to it while she closed her eyes and uttered a silent prayer. Then she dropped the coin. There was no reaction from Big Bertha.

The insatiable machine simply swallowed the dollar. The old lady swayed on the chair, and the guard, afraid that she was about to faint and fall from her perch, prepared himself to catch her. She recovered, however, and reached for her last silver dollar.

Chapter Eighteen

Suddenly there was the shrill sound of a siren, and bright, multicolored lights began to flash on the face of Big Bertha. The old lady jumped back, startled, and surely would have fallen off the chair had not the guard reacted swiftly to stabilize her.

"Oh," she shouted.

Bells began to ring, and silver dollars crashed into the tray that was Big Bertha's belly pouch.

"Oh," the old lady said.

The siren continued its whine as background to the clanging bells and the clattering coins,

215

and the various colored lights still played across the jubilant, triumphant, wrinkled features of the old lady's happy face as she began to cackle uncontrollably. She held her purse below the tray and began to scoop silver dollars into it.

"I won," she shouted. "I did it. I won."

A cheering crowd had gathered around, and its members began to applaud. The excitement of the moment, the loud, mechanical celebration, and the exuberance of the winner all combined proved to be contagious. Onlookers laughed and shouted with her.

"Good going, old gal," shouted the cowboy whose back she had earlier poked with her bony index finger.

"Hooray," shouted another.

The bag was full and heavy, and the tray was empty. The siren droned not as loudly as before, the bells at last became silent, and only a few lights still blinked. The old lady, clutching her coin bag tightly in one gnarled old fist, prepared herself to dismount the chair. The guard moved swiftly to her aid.

"Come along with me, ma'am," he said.

"Where?" she said.

She glared suspiciously at him, pressing the sack of dollars to her withered breasts.

"To get the rest of your money," he said.

"You mean there's more?" she said, her eyes wide in astonished disbelief.

"Sure, lady," he said. "You just hit the big jackpot. A whole million smackers. That's way too many dollars to just drop into the tray. Come along with me now, and we'll get it for you."

She followed the guard through the large and crowded casino to a back room, where she was seated at a long table with two men in gray suits. The guard stood waiting at the door.

"Congratulations," said one of the gray-suited men, a wide grin pasted on his face. "You hit the big one. I'm Victor Brice, the manager here. This is Mr. Grabo with the IRS."

"IRS?" she said. "What's that?"

"The Internal Revenue Service," said Grabo, an undertaker's simpering smile on his pasty face. "We get ours up front."

He rubbed his palms together greedily, as if the money he was about to collect would go into his own private bank account.

"And you are . . . ?" asked Brice.

"I'm the winner," said the old lady.

"Yes," said Brice. "We know that. We need to have your name."

"Why?" she asked. "I won the money. Give it to me."

"We know you won it, but we have to have your name before we can give it to you," he said.

"I won it," she said. "Just give it to me."

"I'm afraid it isn't that simple," said Brice.

"There are laws we have to abide by. We need your name."

"Give me my money," the old lady snarled.

"Don't get excited, lady," said Brice. "All we need is your name, social security number, and a driver's license or some other form of ID. We fill out a couple of forms, Mr. Grabo here gets the government's share, and we write you out a check for the rest. Okay?"

"No," the old lady shouted, standing up from her chair. "It's not okay. I won, and you owe me money. Give it to me. I want my money now."

Grabo rolled his eyes up toward the ceiling and sighed loudly, as Brice looked nervously toward the guard standing at the door.

"Merle," said Brice.

"Yes, sir?" the guard answered, taking a step forward.

"We seem to have a problem here," said Brice. "Go get the cops."

"Yes, sir," Merle said. "I knew there was something wrong with that old broad."

Merle turned to follow his instructions, but the old lady was at the door in a flash and had knocked Merle aside and shoved the latch into its locked position before the three men in the room could react. She stayed at the door with her back to them, and they watched wide-eyed, mesmerized, as her body began to grow. As hairy muscle filled the old lady's clothes, they were ripped asunder and fell from her back, and there on its hind legs at the door stood a snarling puma.

"Oh, my God," Merle shouted.

He reached for his side arm, but the puma turned and pounced on him. Merle screamed as he fell back hard to the floor under the weight and the impact of the great cat. He felt the long, sharp claws dig into his shoulders, and he felt and smelled the hot, foul cat breath as the gaping jaws moved closer to his face. He saw the yellow fangs protruding from the black gums, dripping saliva. He screamed, and then the scream was muffled as the beast closed its jaws around his face.

Brice and Grabo had backed themselves against the far wall. Grabo's face had gone ashen white, and he was trembling violently. His teeth chattered with his fright. Brice decided to go for the door. He scrambled across the table, made a dive for the door, and had just touched the bolt with his hand when he felt the claws rake him down the back. His jacket, vest, and shirt were shredded, and deep trenches in the flesh of his back ran red.

He shouted in pain and terror. His body was pressed against the door by the weight and strength of the cat. He could hear a frantic pounding on the door from the other side.

"Help! Help!" he screamed. Then the fangs bit

into his neck and shoulders from behind.

"Open up," someone yelled from outside. "Open the door. What's going on in there?"

The puma turned in the room, Brice dangling from its powerful jaws. With a mighty shake of its head, it flung the lifeless body across the table and hard into the quivering tax man. With the blood of Brice splattered on his face and chest, the puma easing itself casually up onto the tabletop and moving deliberately toward him, its eyes fixed upon him, its rumbling purr resounding in the room, Grabo began to shriek hysterically.

"Come on," said Shelby. "Let us through here."

The crowd in the casino was packed into the back, near the room where the slaughter had taken place. Their morbid curiosity was doomed to disappointment, however, because the Las Vegas police had the room tightly secured. It took some struggling, but Shelby, Kay, Green, and Chase made their way through the mob, only to find it blocked then by the tight police cordon.

"That's as far as you go," said one of the uniformed cops.

"We're here on official business," said Chase, digging out his badge and holding it up in front of the cop.

"That's not official here," the cop said.

A detective in a rumpled suit with a cigar in his mouth looked out the door of the secured room.

"Shuler," he called out. "Hey, Shuler. Let those four people through."

The cop gave a shrug.

"Yes, sir, Lieutenant Barnaby," he said.

He stepped slightly aside to let them pass.

"Just these four now," he said to the crowd. "Stay back. The rest of you people move on back now. Give us some room here. Move back."

Chase and the others edged their way through the cordon. Chase was the first in the slaughter room. Shelby followed. Quickly taking in the gruesome scene, he put out his arm to block Kay's entrance.

"Kay," he said, "wait outside."

She had already gotten a quick glimpse of the gore inside, and she turned back on her own.

"I will," she said, stepping to just outside the door to lean against the wall.

"Good God," Chase said.

"What the hell brought you here so quick, anyhow?" said Barnaby.

"Hell, Barnaby," said Chase, "the damn story was all over the television. Shit. We've been trying to keep this thing quiet."

"Yeah?" said Barnaby. "Well, I think you'd better tell me about it now."

Robert J. Conley

"I'm not authorized to do that," Chase said. "What happened here?"

"Who knows?" said Barnaby, throwing up his arms. "Look around. Just look at this shit. How the hell would anyone know what happened in here?"

"Somebody knows something," said Shelby.

"Barnaby," said Chase, "why don't you give General Niles another call? Or I can call him for you. He can fill you in if he wants to, but I know he'll tell you again to cooperate with us."

"Oh, hell," said Barnaby. "All right. I don't need to call the fucking general again. I called him once, and I called the goddamned Pentagon to check up on him. I've already been told to kiss your ass. Okay? Okay. Here's the story. A little old lady hit the Jackpot on Big Bertha out there."

"What's Big Bertha?" asked Chase.

"A big slot machine," Barnaby answered. "It paid off big—a million bucks, so they brought her back here to get her name, social security number, and ID. The tax man is back here to collect Uncle Sam's share, and the casino pays off the rest with a check. That's standard procedure for a big win like that.

"Well, grandma gets in the room with the manager, the security guard, and the fed. The door's closed. The next thing anybody outside knows, they're screaming in here. They can't break in. Someone has bolted the door from the inside. One guy says he heard something sounded like a lion or a tiger. We broke in the door when we got here. It's a mess in here, as you can well see, but we're pretty sure we got the remains of the three guys here.

"There's no sign of the old lady. Well, that is, except for these rags. That's what's left of her clothes, and this bag of silver dollars. That was hers. Now, you tell me what the fuck happened here, Chase. You tell me. Did somebody's granny do this? Is she running around Vegas naked? Did she growl like a goddamned lion? And how the hell did she get out of the room and leave the damn door locked? You tell me."

"It's Brass," said Shelby. "It's got to be."

"Who?" said Barnaby. "Brass? What's this brass shit?"

Jim Green was staring at the gore all around the room. He hadn't said a word since their arrival on the scene. Chase, glancing over toward Shelby following his last remark, noticed Green. He put a hand on Shelby's shoulder and leaned in close.

"Take Green out of here, will you?" he said in a low voice. "This is the first time he's seen this. Get your wife too, and the three of you go on back over to the room. All right? I'll be along later. I'm going to go ahead and fill Barnaby in on the whole thing. I don't know what Niles would say, but I can't just leave him like this. He's got to know the whole story."

"Yeah, sure," said Shelby. He stepped over to Green's side. "Hey, buddy," he said, "let's get out of here. What do you say?"

He had killed again, and that eased a little of the pain and humiliation of the tremendous reversal of fortune he had just suffered, but the sting remained. His pride was sorely wounded. He had been coldly robbed of what was rightfully his, cheated of the fortune he had worked so hard and plotted so carefully to acquire. What did he know of those things they had demanded of him anyway? Cards, numbers, IRS, ID.

For the first time since his recent joyful emergence into this utterly changed world, Brass realized with a terrible fear and emptiness just how helpless he really was, how alone, how ignorant and therefore vulnerable. He huddled, naked, hugging his knees to his chest, in his own rightful form, in a dark alley, back against a brick wall, in the comforting shadow of a large metal box filled with trash.

He had thought to return to Judith Ann, his pockets bulging with the heavy, silver coins, their futures secure in this world of money. Now he had no money. He had used it all for the sake of his grand scheme, and the scheme had worked. It had worked, and then they had stolen the prize from him at the last, glorious instant.

In the form he had been forced to take in order to creep out of the room under the door after having slaughtered the thieves, he had been much too tiny to even think of dragging the bag containing the coins that had dropped from the guts of Big Bertha.

The longer he sat, the more he despaired, and the despair led to hatred, and the combination of deep despondency and bitter rancor caused spasms deep down in his bowels that drove upward in his system until the salt water ran from his red and swollen eyes down his cheeks in rivulets.

He opened his mouth wide to suck in air in an effort to defeat the spasms, and the hot tears ran into his mouth. He tasted them with his tongue, and the taste of the salt water there in the cold, dank darkness of the alley reminded him of the wet prison he had so recently escaped, and he roared, his agonized, resonant wail resounding and reverberating in the penumbra of the narrow closure in which he cowered.

Chapter Nineteen

Judith Ann had seen the same television news report that had propelled Shelby and his companions to the casino that had been the site of the carnage. She knew that her "John Brass" had gone to that very casino, and the news report had informed her that the one-million-dollar Jackpot had indeed been won.

However, it had been won by a little old lady. Judith Ann had seen her on the videotape of the win. She had seen no sign of Brass on that tape. The news story had gone on to describe a terrible and mysterious slaughter that had taken place in a back room of the casino almost immediately following the big win.

The old lady had vanished, and the million dollars went unclaimed. The manager of the casino, a security guard, and an IRS man had apparently been brutally killed. There was no word of Brass. No sign. But Judith Ann had a feeling that he had somehow been involved. He had not returned to the hotel room. He had been gone all night long.

Judith Ann was afraid. She was alone, broke, and hungry. There was something else bothering her too, but she tried not to think about it, not to put it into words. She knew, though, that she would have to find out. She would have to know one way or the other soon. But it was just too crazy. She told herself that it couldn't be. It was way too soon.

She made some hasty plans, opened the telephone book to the yellow pages, and found the telephone number and street address of a local free clinic. She ripped the page from the book and stuffed it into her purse. Then she quickly packed her small but new wardrobe and for the second time slipped out of a hotel by a back door without paying her bill.

It was daylight, and he had resumed the now familiar, even comfortable shape of John Brass. He had shaken off his despondency and would go back to the room to tell Judith Ann what had happened. It would be all right. He would get more money. He would come up with another plan, something to hold them over for a while.

Judith Ann would tell him how to get the cards and numbers, and then he could find out again when Big Bertha was due to pay off big bucks. Last night need not be thought of as a disaster, he decided. He would think of it instead as merely a test run, a trial, a big experiment. He had learned from the experience, too. For now he knew that he needed cards, cards with numbers on them. So he would get cards and numbers, and then he would make another assault on Big Bertha.

He walked into the hotel lobby and over to the elevator. He liked the elevators. Some things about this new world were fun and exciting. He thrilled at the sensation in his stomach as the little box carried him up to the floor on which his Judith Ann awaited him. He hurried to the room and opened the door with his key. Judith Ann was not there. He called out to her.

"Judith Ann. Judith Ann, where are you?"

He looked in the bathroom but found it unoccupied. She was just not there. He asked himself where she could be.

"She went to get a Coke," he said out loud, "or something to eat."

But he remembered then that she had given

him all of their money to use on Big Bertha. She would have nothing with which to buy a Coke or food. Then he noticed the clothes rack. The only clothes hanging there were his. He jerked open the dresser drawers. Again he found only his own things. He looked around the room in quick movements for the suitcase, which, by this time, he expected not to find. It, too, was gone.

"She left," he said, standing stupidly in the middle of the room, talking to himself and suddenly feeling very much alone. "She's left me."

"You can wait in here, Judith Ann," said the nurse. "Dr. Garwood will be right in. Just have a seat right here."

Judith Ann sat down in the chair, which stood centered in front of the desk, so that the person who sat in it would be facing directly the one who sat behind the desk. It was a small office, and Judith Ann began to feel just a bit claustrophobic. She had already felt sick to her stomach. She had felt sick even before she found her way to the clinic, but waiting alone there in the tiny office, she wasn't at all certain whether she still felt sick from earlier, or if the intimate and offensive examination had made her sick all over again.

The examination and the worrying about its results. She had initially been glad to discover that Dr. Garwood was female, but during the actual examination, she hadn't been so sure. It seemed strange to her, even perverse, yes, to have a woman probing around so deeply into her private parts. *Bitch*, she thought. Well, the doctor would be in soon and tell her that everything was all right. That was all she could say, wasn't it? Judith Ann felt foolish for even having worried about it, for coming here in the first place. There was just no way. There hadn't been enough time for that to have happened to her.

She wondered what Don and her mother were doing just now, and then she wondered why she had wondered. At last Dr. Garwood came into the room and sat down behind the desk. Judith Ann wondered if she had washed her hands. The doctor opened a manila folder that lay there before her on the desk, studied it for a moment in silence, then looked up across the desk.

"Judith Ann?" she said.

"Yeah?" said the girl.

"You're sixteen years old?" asked the doctor.

"Yeah," Judith Ann said.

"And your parents are in California?"

"Uh-huh," said Judith Ann. "Well, one of them is."

"Oh, I see," said Dr. Garwood.

Judith Ann sat looking at her own lap.

"Do they know where you are?" the doctor asked.

Judith Ann ducked her head even more and sat silent.

"Well," said the doctor, adjusting the glasses on her nose, "it's our policy here not to contact your parents unless you want us to, so you don't have to worry about that. We don't call the police either."

"Yeah, I know," Judith Ann said. "I asked first."

Dr. Garwood sighed. She looked at Judith Ann, but all she could see was the top of the girl's head. She had seen so many like this one. Why did they all have to learn the hard way?

"Well," she said, "I'm afraid that your fears were well founded, Judith Ann. You are pregnant."

"For sure?" Judith Ann said. She wanted to tell the damn doctor that it couldn't be. There just hadn't been enough time. There had only been John Brass. No one else. No one before that.

"There's no doubt about it," the doctor said. "It's still early enough that you could have an abortion, if you want, or you could have the child and have it put up for adoption. You're not married?"

"No," said Judith Ann. "Well, not exactly."

"Is your boyfriend with you?"

"He's gone."

Judith Ann stared at the desk in front of her, avoiding contact with the doctor's eyes, and the image that floated in her mind was an image of John Brass. He was a strange one, all right. Where in the hell had he come from, anyway? He was like a child in some ways. There were so many things he didn't know about, it was almost unbelievable. But then in some other ways . . . Like, how had he killed Leon? Did he kill those people in the casino? And just how in the hell had he done this to her? Who was John Brass? What was he? Her thoughts were interrupted by the doctor's next question.

"Do you know what you want to do, Judith Ann?" said Dr. Garwood. "We can try to help you, if we know what you want."

Judith Ann tried to think of an answer for the doctor. What did she want? She didn't know, except that she wanted Brass to come back. She wondered why he had left her. Was he in trouble? Did he have anything to do with that mess at the casino? The killings? She didn't care. He had killed Leon. She knew that. She'd known it all along. She didn't know how he had done it, but she was sure that he had. And that other guy, the one who had owned the old Ford. If Brass hadn't gotten into some kind of trouble, then he had simply left her, gotten tired of her. And now, as incredible as it seemed, she was pregnant, almost like by magic, and her baby would have to grow up without its father.

"I'm hungry," she said, "and I don't have any money."

Dr. Garwood opened a desk drawer and took out a small card on which she scribbled something. Then she handed it across the desk to Judith Ann.

"Go to this address," she said, "and give them this card. They'll give you something to eat. If I can help any more, let me know."

It was the same man he had chased away from Big Bertha the night of the experiment, but this night the man was at a table with other people, throwing little pieces of bone with black dots on them. The game was similar to one he could remember from long ago, hundreds, perhaps thousands of years past, but he could not quite grasp its details.

He could tell, though, that the man was winning. After he had watched for a while from a discreet distance, he saw the man quit playing and pick up a great pile of coins of a type Brass had not seen before. They were about the size of the heavy dollars, but they didn't clink the same way, and they were red and white and blue.

He watched as the man walked through the crowd to a window at the back of the room and gave the colorful coins to a woman there. Then the woman gave him several pieces of the green paper money, which Brass knew about, as he had seen it before. The man put the money into his billfold, stuffed the billfold into his back pocket and tipped his hat to the woman behind the window. Then he headed toward the front door of the casino. He was leaving.

As the Texan got into his big Lincoln, he didn't see the figure lurking in the shadows of the parking lot, failed to notice it watching to see which car he would get into, was unaware when it skulked up behind and metamorphosed itself into something less noticeable yet far more formidable, something that could climb undetected onto the trunk lid from behind and slither its way to the top of the car to ride along with him, unknown to him, just above his head, something that waited patiently for its opportunity to strike.

The Texan parked the Lincoln in another parking lot, this one surrounding a large, modern motel on the outskirts of the city. He parked off to one side. It was late, and the lot was nearly filled with cars but almost empty of human life. It was not quite dark, for lamps on tall poles cast a hazy light over the blacktop pavement and the tops of the various automobiles.

Around the dimly glowing globes, hundreds of summer insects swarmed in orbit.

The Texan shut off his engine, pulled the key from the ignition switch, and opened the door. As he put his left foot out onto the pavement and leaned his body out to crawl out of the car, a flash of movement brushed past his face. A heavy weight fell on his shoulders. Something strong, powerfully strong, speedily slipped its way around his neck and shoulders.

He grabbed at it, tried to scream for help, but in an instant it was crushing him, pressing out his breath and his strength. Only pitiful gagging sounds would come out of his mouth. He fell out onto the pavement still struggling, but more weakly. His tongue swelled and protruded from his mouth. He could feel his eyeballs trying to pop out of their sockets. His lungs tried to convulse for want of air, but they were squeezed too tightly even for that. He had one final, feverish thought flash through his brain before his right leg gave a little kick, and he ceased to move. *Boa constrictor*.

"Damn it," said Chase. "It's the same thing as last time."

"No," said Shelby. "Hell no. It's worse. They were right here. Right down the hall from us. Right down there in that room."

"They got a little smarter," said Kay. "They

didn't use the name Brass this time."

"It had to be them," said Shelby. "Had to be. Young girl did the registering. Desk clerks never got more than a glimpse of the man. They sneaked out without paying their bill."

"Nothing left behind in the room except Coke cans," said Kay.

The telephone rang, and Chase jerked up the receiver.

"Yeah?" he said.

For the rest of the conversation, he only repeated that same word three or four more times. Then he hung up the phone.

"Well?" said Kay.

"The fingerprints found in the room here," said Chase, "just the one set again, match those found in the other room. It was them, all right. No other match has been found. We've got prints, but nothing to match them up with."

"And now that they've started using different names," said Shelby, "it won't do us any good to check hotel registrations. Shit."

"The local cops are trying to put together an artist's conception of what the girl looks like," Chase said, "based on descriptions from the desk clerks. We can circulate that drawing when we get it."

"What else can we do?" asked Kay.

"Nothing," said Chase. "Not a goddamned

thing. Just wait for a break or wait for him to make another move."

"God help us," said Shelby. "I hate to think what that might be."

Throughout that entire discussion, Jim Green sat staring blankly at the carpet on the floor.

He dragged the lifeless body through the parking lot between cars until he came to the steel Dumpster. There he quickly emptied out its pockets, flung it over the side into the big box, and conjured up an imitation of its clothes. They were neatly pressed, though, not like the rumpled ones, stained from the crushing.

And it was like a resurrection. It was as if the tall Texan, so recently and rudely robbed of his life, lived and breathed and walked again. He put the billfold in his hip pocket and in his trouser pockets some loose change and some keys—car keys, he was sure. He held out another key, one he recognized as a room key. He had not learned either letters or numbers, but he knew that the scratchings on the key would match those on the door to a room inside. He went into the motel through a side door and found the room with surprisingly little trouble.

He opened the door and stepped inside. No one was there. He looked at the clothes rack and found it full of clothes on hangers. He opened the dresser drawers and found them full. He turned on the television set, took the billfold from his pocket, and sat on the edge of the bed. Then he took the money out and tossed it onto the bed beside him.

He had a whole pile of green money of different kinds. He couldn't read the numbers, but he knew that some of them were worth more than others. He was rich, he decided. He would be all right. If Judith Ann had not run away from him, she could have been rich too. It was her own fault, he told himself, that she wasn't there to share it with him.

He stood up and looked in the mirror behind the dresser, and he saw the man he had followed and killed. He no longer saw the man Judith Ann had known as John Brass, and that made it easier to shove her on out of his mind. He was no longer the man who had lost Judith Ann. He was somebody else entirely. And what's more, he thought gleefully, going back to the billfold, he was a man with cards and numbers. He would repeat his earlier trick with Big Bertha until he once again knew when she would pay off big. Then with his new body, new clothes, and new cards and numbers, he would make this new man rich indeed.

Chapter Twenty

Shelby slept fitfully beside Kay in the hotel room. His dreams were haunted by visions of giants made of brass who alternately became spiders, monstrous, drooling grizzly bears, lions, slavering vicious dogs, and assorted other frightful monstrosities. Rooms were filled with blood, and various body parts floated past. He saw the monster ravishing a child as she screamed for help. She called his name.

"Shelby," she cried. "Shelby. Help me."

Desperate and trembling, he got up from the bed, wearing only his shorts, and he went to her aid, but he could no longer see either her or the great brass freak. He was alone in a vast chamber with a shining, slick tile floor. He walked slowly and apprehensively ahead, not knowing where he was going, feeling the cold, hard floor with his bare feet.

From somewhere up ahead, blood began to pour out across the floor. Hot and sticky, it washed over his bare feet, carrying with it bits of flesh, pieces of entrails. Shelby stepped on something slimy, and he started to slip. Terror gripped him deep inside his guts. He screamed, and he woke up. He sat up straight in the bed, perspiring heavily. Kay was awake and sitting up there beside him.

"Are you all right?" she said.

Her arms went around him, and she pulled his head to her breast.

"Yeah," he said. "I'm okay," but he realized that he felt immensely comforted by her mothering caress, and he reached his arms around her torso and held himself tightly to her.

"I'm all right," he said again. "Just—just a bad dream. That's all."

"Joe," she said, "we're doing all we can."

"Yeah," he said. "I know."

He had stopped trembling, calmed down some, and he pulled himself loose from the embrace to sit up straight again. He could feel the sheet beneath him wet with his sweat.

"It's just that I—I feel so guilty—so damn . . . responsible," he said.

"That's silly," she said. "It's not your fault. It's no one's fault. It just happened, and you're trying to do something about it. Some men would just run away from it—ignore it and hope that it would go away—or hope that someone else would take care of it."

Shelby stood up and walked to the center of the room, then turned back to face Kay. He didn't know if she would understand—could ever understand. He rubbed his face hard with both hands, then ran his hands through his hair.

"Kay," he said, "what do you know of the history of the Corps? The United States Army Corps of Engineers? Do you know how many projects the Corps has had over the years on Indian land? On reservations or other land owned by Indians or Indian tribes? How many of their homes we've flooded with dam projects? How many families we've uprooted and relocated? Do you have any idea of the number of times Indian people have told us, warned us, begged us even, not to go ahead with a project, and how many times we've ignored them? That old man, he told me not to go on with that project on the beach. He said it was a bad place.

"God, if we'd only learned to listen somewhere along the line, this—this thing that's go-

Robert J. Conley

ing on would never have happened. All those people—Bud and the others—they'd all be alive. Ten people killed, maybe more that we don't know about, and that young girl—God knows what's happened to her. Is this the only way we can learn a lesson?"

"Oh Lord," said Kay, "I hope not. I surely hope not."

The tall Texan dressed himself in a clean suit, high, polished boots and a broad-brimmed, clean, white hat. He drove the Lincoln back into the heart of the city and parked it alongside the curb. Then he got out to walk the streets of Las Vegas. The money in his pockets made him itch for action, but he knew now that he must be careful. He did not know what the different bills were worth, and he did not know the rules for the wide variety of gambling games, all of which were new to him.

Besides all that, he was hungry. He came upon a place where he saw through the window people eating, and he stood on the sidewalk and watched through the window for a moment or two. He wanted to go in, but he knew that the food cost money, and he was afraid that in his ignorance, he would give himself away when it came time to pay.

He walked on. Up ahead, shuffling toward him on the sidewalk, was a man in dirty disarray. He was a small man with stubble on his face, a furtive, weasely-looking little man. The tall Texan thought for an instant that he would step to one side to avoid dirtying his clothes by a chance brushing against the pathetic creature. Then he decided that it would be better to make the dirty little man step aside. As they passed each other, the little man suddenly clutched at the Texan's coat sleeve.

"Hey, wait up, cowboy," he said.

The tall Texan looked down at the little man.

"Let go," he said.

The man turned loose of the sleeve but pressed around to block the Texan's path.

"Okay," he said. "Okay, cowboy. Whatever you say."

"What's this cowboy?" said the Texan, who, of course, was Brass. "Are you insulting me?"

"No. Hell no, mister," said the little man. "I wouldn't do that. I just thought that you was a cowboy, you know, because of your clothes. If I insulted you, I apologize all to hell. God damn, hell, I'm broke and out here begging in the streets. I ain't going to insult a body who looks like he might lend me a hand, now am I?"

"I guess not," Brass said.

"Could you see your way to letting me have a few bucks?" the little man whined. "I'm hungry as all hell. I ain't had a bite to eat in four days, mister. Honest to God, I ain't. I don't even live here. Come out from Chanutte, Kansas, and had a run of bad luck. I could sure use a little help."

"Get out of my way," said Brass.

The little man stepped aside as Brass walked on ahead.

"Well, just pardon me all to hell," he called out, "you rich son of a bitch. I'm sorry I dirtied your breathing space. Just excuse the shit out of me. Goddamn."

Brass stopped abruptly and turned around, and the panhandler felt the urge to turn and run. Something held him in place.

"Wait a minute," Brass said.

He walked back toward the street bum, who still stood poised to duck or to run, whichever might seem appropriate when the time came.

"Can you read?" Brass asked him.

"What?" the little man said.

"I said can you read?"

"What the hell kind of a question is that to ask a man in the street?" the bum said. "Can I read?"

"You want money, don't you?" said Brass. "I have lots of money. Can you read?"

"Hell, yeah, I can read," the little man said. "I went to school. I ain't been this way all my life. I told you, I come up here from Chanutte, Kansas, and I just had a run of bad luck. I may be dirt poor right now, but I ain't ignorant. Shit. Can I read?"

"So you can read?" Brass asked.

"Yeah," said the man. "Hell, I just said so, didn't I?"

"Are you hungry?"

"Hell yeah. I just said that too. Hungry? Man, I can feel my backbone through my goddamned belly."

"Let's go," said Brass. "I'll buy us some food."

They walked together back to the place Brass had stared into a few moments earlier, went inside, and sat down at a booth.

"You tell them what we want," Brass said.

"You want me to order for the both of us?" the little man said.

"Yes," said Brass.

A waitress appeared and put two glasses of water on the table.

"You want to see menus?" she asked.

"Yeah," said the weaselly man. "And we want coffee. Lots of coffee."

She tossed down the menus and left. The two men picked up the menus and opened them.

"You got that upside down," said the little man.

Brass turned his menu over.

Soon they were eating steak and potatoes. The panhandler could scarcely believe the situation he had blundered into.

"Fine meal," he said, talking with his mouth full. "Fine and dandy. I do appreciate it, Mr.— Say, what's your name? What do I call you?"

Brass sipped his coffee and looked over the rim of the cup at the shifty eyes of the other man.

"I don't know," he said. "That's what I'm going to pay you for. What's your name?"

"You don't know your own name?" the bum said, incredulous.

"Keep your voice down," Brass said. "You heard me. What's your name?"

"Hiram," said the little man. "Hiram Fishgall, from Chanutte, Kansas."

Brass leaned back and laughed out loud. Hiram Fishgall stopped eating, though he still had food in his mouth.

"What's so funny?" he asked.

"You smell like fish," said Brass. "When we finish here, we'll go to my room and get you cleaned up, but first we'll stop and get you some new clothes."

Fishgall didn't like having his name laughed at, or being told that he smelled bad, but when he heard that he was about to get new clothes, he decided to take it all good-naturedly. He chuckled, a forced chuckle, and some half-chewed beef dropped from his mouth.

*　　*　　*

When they had finished their meal, and the waitress had left the bill on the table, Brass pulled the wallet from his hip pocket and held it open under Fishgall's nose.

"Good goddamn Lord a'mighty," said Fishgall.

"Which one do you need to pay for this?" Brass asked.

Fishgall reached tentatively for a bill. When he saw that Brass wasn't going to snatch the wallet away or do him any violence, he deftly removed one. He thought for an instant of pulling out a large bill, lying, and pocketing the change, but he wasn't at all sure that he wasn't being set up by this strange acting cowboy. How could anyone who looked like that, dressed like that, and had that much money be so damn dumb? He decided to play it straight. He paid the bill, threw a couple of one-dollar bills on the table, and gave Brass the rest of the change.

"What's that for?" asked Brass, looking at the bills on the table.

"Tip," said Fishgall.

"Tip?" said Brass.

"For the waitress," Fishgall said. "For serving us."

"Oh," Brass said. "Okay."

They found a clothing store and bought Fishgall some new clothes, then Brass led the way to the Lincoln.

"Got yourself a parking ticket," said Fishgall.

"What's that?" Brass asked.

Fishgall pulled the ticket out from under the wiper blade and waved it under Brass's nose.

"This here," he said. "That's what."

"What is it?" Brass asked.

"You didn't put enough money in the meter," said Fishgall. "Now you got a damn ticket."

"I don't understand," said Brass. "What's it for?"

Fishgall took a deep breath in preparation for a long explanation, but then he hesitated. He felt like some kind of a fool. Did this man really not know what a parking ticket was? Well, he had gotten a new set of clothes and a good meal so far. He would play along.

"It costs money to park your car," he said. "You put it in here. If you don't, or if you don't put enough, or if you park too long, they give you a ticket. This here thing. Then you have to pay even more."

"Oh," said Brass. "I see. Where do I pay?"

"The ticket?" said Fishgall.

"Where do I pay for the ticket?" Brass said.

Fishgall turned the ticket over to see what was written there.

"Well," he said, "you can put the money right in here. See? The ticket is also an envelope. You can put the money right in here and drop it in

248

one of them yellow boxes on the meters. There's one—right down yonder."

Brass pulled out his billfold again and handed it to Fishgall.

"Pay it," he said.

Shelby jumped up to answer the knock at the door.

"Barnaby," he said. "Come on in."

The detective walked into the room and nodded greetings to its other three occupants.

"Hello, Mr. Barnaby," said Kay.

"Ma'am," said Barnaby through teeth clenched around his short cigar. "I'll come right to the point. We got a call from the city sanitation department. One of those trucks that empties those big Dumpsters—you know what I mean? They took their load out to the dump and poured it out, and one of the men spotted a body in it. Male, about forty years old. Dressed in cowboy clothes. He'd been crushed to death. The coroner says it looks like it was done by one of those big snakes."

"A constrictor?" said Shelby.

"Yeah," said Barnaby. "One of them. A boa constrictor or something like that."

"Damn," said Chase. "What next?"

"That makes eleven now that we know about for sure," Shelby said.

"This thing has got to be stopped," said Kay.

"It's got to. Somehow. Some way, we've got to stop it."

"What have we got, Barnaby?" asked Chase. "We got anything more than we did? Anything at all?"

"We've got the girl's fingerprints," Barnaby said. "No match for them, though. We got the police drawing done. Took it to both hotel clerks, who remembered seeing the girl. They say it's a good likeness."

He reached into his inside coat pocket and pulled out a copy of the drawing, which he handed to Chase.

"There she is," he said. "I'm having men take copies of this all over town, to hotels and motels, casinos. Nothing so far."

"What about the body?" said Shelby. "The latest victim. Anything on him?"

"No ID," Barnaby said. "His pockets had been emptied. We're checking his prints. Cowboy suit was bought in a store right here in town, boots and hat too, but no one there remembers the guy who bought them. We've got nothing else to go on."

"We're not doing any good here," said Jim Green.

Green had been so quiet lately that Shelby had begun to worry about him. When he spoke up, everyone in the room was surprised, and they all turned to face him.

"We've got to try something different," he said.

"What?" said Chase. "You got any ideas?"

"Let me go to Oklahoma," Green said.

"What for?" Chase asked. "What the hell you going to do there? Brass is here. Right here in Vegas. Somewhere right under our noses. You want to go to Oklahoma?"

"I want to go see an Indian doctor," said Green, "medicine man, you'd call him."

"Oh, come on," said Chase. "What the hell for?"

Shelby stepped quickly up to Chase's side, looking intently at Green. He put a hand on Chase's shoulder.

"Wait a minute, Harvey," he said. "Wait. This whole thing is crazy. You know? I mean, Brass is a character right out of the old Cherokee oral tradition, right? Maybe Jim's right. Let him go."

Chase heaved a sigh and pulled out his Marlboros.

"All right," he said. "Hell, I don't have any better idea just now anyhow."

"Where will I find you when I get back?" Green asked.

"Unless Brass leads us out of town," Chase said, "in which case we'll leave word with Barnaby where we're headed, we'll be right here. Right by God here."

* * *

Judith Ann was full from the free meal, but her feet ached from walking all over the city. She was tired and she felt dirty. She wanted a bath and a place to lie down. She wanted a Coke, but she didn't even have enough money for that. *Pregnant*, she thought. *I'm going to have a baby.* What would her friends think? *I don't have any friends*, she told herself in quick response.

She walked past the lobby of a big hotel, and she thought of the luxurious rooms she had so recently occupied. She thought of the big, soft beds, and she thought of John Brass. Where could he have gone? Why hadn't he come back? She shifted the suitcase from her right hand to her left. It seemed much bigger and heavier now than it had before. She was passing a casino, and she stepped into the doorway. A policeman suddenly blocked her path.

"Sorry," he said. "You can't come in here."

"Why not?" she said.

"You're too young," he said. "I can tell just by looking at you."

"Well," she said, "I'm just looking for someone. That's all. I ain't going to gamble. I don't have any money anyway."

He looked at her, at the suitcase in her hand, and he shook his head a bit.

"Where do you live, kid?" he asked.

"I don't have to tell you that," Judith Ann said. "Do I?"

"You run away from home?" he asked.

"I don't think he's in there anyway," she said. "I guess it was another place he was talking about. I'll just be on my way."

"Wait a minute," said the policeman.

"Are you going to run me in?" she asked.

"Have you broken a law?"

"No."

"Then I guess not," he said. "I just thought you might like to know about a place in town." He pulled a card out of his pocket and started to write on it. "It's a place that helps runaway kids. Here."

"I'm not—"

"I didn't say anything about you," the cop said. "Here. Take it. Just in case."

Judith Ann took the card and hurried on down the sidewalk.

Chapter Twenty-one

On the way to the motel, Fishgall had asked
Brass if he wanted a drink, and he had talked
Brass into stopping at a liquor store where Fishgall, with Brass's money, had purchased a large
jug of red wine. Once in the room, Brass had
not allowed Fishgall to open the jug until he had
bathed and put on the new clothes. Then they
had gotten the glasses out of the bathroom, set
them, with the wine jug, in the middle of the
table, which stood by the window, and sat down
across from each other.

"Now?" said Fishgall.

"Now, Fish," said Brass.

Fishgall opened the jug and poured some wine into the two glasses. He held his up in the manner of a toast.

"Here's to you," he said. "Down the hatch."

He drank it down without a pause and refilled the glass. Brass tasted his.

"It's good," he said.

"Damn right," said Fishgall. "Drink it on down."

Brass did, and Fishgall refilled the glasses. Brass pulled out his billfold and tossed it on the table in front of Fishgall.

"Now," he said, "tell me who I am."

Fishgall gave Brass a puzzled look.

"Take out the cards," said Brass, "and tell me who I am."

Fishgall pulled all the cards out of the billfold. He found a Texas driver's license, social security card, and various credit cards. The driver's license had a picture on it. Fishgall looked at it and then at Brass.

"Well?" said Brass.

"You're Vernon Gardiner," said Fishgall. "Hell, you knew that. You're testing me. Didn't think I could really read, did you? Vernon Gardiner. See?"

He poured two more glasses of wine.

"Vernon Gardiner," said Brass. He took a

drink of his wine. "Vernon Gardiner. Good. Now tell me about the money."

Fishgall took all the bills out and began to sort them. He made a stack of ones, a stack of fives, tens, twenties, fifties, and hundreds. The amount of money he was handling nearly took away his breath. He drained his glass and re-filled it.

"Do you have any change?" he said.

"Change?" said Brass.

"Coins," said Fishgall. "Change. Pocket money. The kind that jingles, you know?"

Brass stood up and reached into a pocket of his trousers. He pulled out a handful of change and dumped it on the table. Fishgall sorted it as he had the bills, Brass watching keenly his every move. Fishgall picked up a penny.

"Now," he said, "you see this here?"

"Of course I see it," said Brass.

"This here penny," said Fishgall, "is the littlest money we got. It ain't worth much. You get five of these, and it's equal to this one here. This one's a nickel. Understand?"

Brass counted out five pennies and then picked up a nickel.

"Five pennies is the same as one nickel," he said. "Yes. Go on."

Fishgall refilled the glasses and picked up a dime.

*   *   *

Brass made Fishgall go through the money twice, from the penny to the hundred-dollar bill, and then count hundreds up to thousands. Then he went through it once again for himself.

"By God, Mr. Gardiner," said Fishgall, "you're a quick study, you are. You got that down pat."

It was a good thing, too, for Brass was beginning to feel woozy.

"How much is here?" he said. "How much all together?"

"Four thousand and something," said Fishgall, his voice beginning to slur just a little.

"How much exactly?" said Brass, speaking loudly.

Fishgall fumbled through the money again.

"Four thousand three hundred and fifty-seven dollars and seventy-seven cents," he said at last.

"Am I rich, Fishguts?" Brass asked.

"Fishgall," shouted Fishgall.

Brass laughed.

"Fishguts," he said. "Am I rich?"

"You're a rich son of a bitch," Fishgall said, and he joined in the laughter.

"Rich son of a bitch," shouted Brass.

"Do I get the job?" Fishgall asked.

"Job?" Brass said.

"Do I work for you?"

"Yes," Brass roared. "Fishguts works for me—for Vernon Gardiner. Rich Vernon Gardiner. Rich son of a bitch."

Fishgall poured two more glasses of wine, and he and Brass each took a long drink.

"When do I get paid?" Fishgall asked.

Brass reached for the money on the table and clutched a handful of bills. Without looking to see what he had picked up, he tossed the bills toward Fishgall.

"Here, Fishguts," he said. "Here's your money. Fishguts, how much is a million?"

"I don't know," said Fishgall, gathering up the bills Brass had thrown at him. "It's a whole lot, though."

"More than a thousand?"

"A whole lot more."

Brass laughed some more. He thought that the room had begun to spin. He felt strange, and when he stood up, his legs were wobbly.

"Fishguts," he said. "I'm dizzy."

"You're drunk," said Fishgall, laughing. "So am I."

"Drunk?" said Brass.

"Ain't you ever been drunk before?"

"I don't know drunk," Brass said.

"You are drunk," said Fishgall. "Hell, that's what you are. Drunk. That's what we drink this stuff for. To get drunk."

"Drunk," said Brass. "Drunk. I'm drunk. It feels funny. Silly. It feels good."

"It's what life is all about," said Fishgall.

"More wine," shouted Brass.

Fishgall lifted the jug.

"It's all gone," he said.

"Then get some money," Brass said, "and let's go get some more."

Fishgall stuffed some money into his pocket, and they left the room together, staggering down the hallway, weaving from wall to wall. Out in the parking lot, Fishgall stumbled and fell, and Brass roared with laughter. Fishgall got back on his feet.

"Not so loud," he said. "Someone'll call the cops."

"What for?" Brass asked.

"Lock us up for being drunk," said Fishgall.

"Cops don't like drunk?" Brass asked.

"Hell no," said Fishgall. "Cops hate drunks. They'll get us for sure, if we ain't careful. Be careful."

Brass lowered his voice to a near whisper.

"Be careful," he said.

They made it to the Lincoln, and Brass fumbled in his pockets for the keys.

"Can you drive drunk?" asked Fishgall.

"Don't know," said Brass. "Never been drunk before."

"You better let me drive, then," Fishgall said. "Hell, I drive better drunk than sober."

Brass tossed the keys at Fishgall, who dropped them onto the pavement and nearly fell over picking them up. Brass laughed again, then caught himself.

"Be careful," he whispered. "You drive, Fishguts. Let's get more wine."

Fishgall brought the Lincoln's engine to a roaring start, jammed the gearshift lever into reverse, and squealed the tires as he backed into another car. He hit the brakes, a bit late, and shifted into drive.

"Oops," he said.

Brass giggled.

"I'm just not used to this car," said Fishgall.

He managed to get to the liquor store, go inside and buy another jug of wine, and drive back to the motel without hitting anything again and without getting stopped, in spite of the fact that he often wandered into the wrong lane and caused several other motorists to lean on their horns as they passed. Back in the hotel, they tried to walk straight and stay quiet on their way back to the room, but they staggered, stumbled, and giggled the whole way. Back inside the room, the door shut, Brass relaxed again.

"Pour wine," he shouted.

Fishgall poured two glasses, and they drained them at once. Brass slapped Fishgall on the chest, knocking him back onto one of the beds.

"We're drunk, Fishguts," he said, and he fell back onto the other bed in a fit of laughter.

Holding his stomach, he rolled from side to side until he fell off onto the floor on the side of the bed away from Fishgall's vision. Fishgall crept up, got the jug, then took it, with his glass, back to the bed with him. Brass's laughter had stopped.

"You want another drink, Mr. Gardiner?" Fishgall asked.

Fishgall heard no response from Brass.

"Must have passed out," he mumbled as he poured one for himself. He thought about getting up to see if the Texan had indeed passed out. If so, he thought, he could take all the money and get the hell out. But he still had in the back of his mind the thought that perhaps this Vernon Gardiner was playing him for some kind of fool, or testing him, or something. He might simply be pretending to be passed out in order to catch him trying to steal the money.

Then too, four thousand dollars, though a lot to a man when he's broke, wasn't really all that much money. Fishgall thought that Gardiner must have much more than that. If he stuck with Gardiner, kept his new job, whatever it might be, he might eventually see much more than the four thousand. But the thing that really made up Fishgall's mind for him to stay in the room was that he was comfortable on the bed, with his glass and his jug, and he was too drunk to think seriously about trying to run away from anything.

"Mr. Gardiner?" he said.

A rat crawled out from under the other bed and stared at Fishgall. It crawled across the floor and scratched at the side of the bed. Fishgall heard the scratching and looked down. He screamed. The rat gripped the bedcoverings in an attempt to crawl up on the bed with him. He screamed again and stood up on the bed. Then he threw the jug, missing the rat, but causing it to run back under the other bed. The jug was smashed on the floor. Fishgall kept standing on the mattress, pressing himself back against the wall and making little whimpering noises. He looked around the room and saw no sign of the rat. It must be under one of the beds.

"Mr. Gardiner," he shouted.

He decided that he would have to get down onto the floor and go for Gardiner, try to wake him up. He would brave it. He stepped down slowly, cautiously, and stood still for a moment, half expecting to be attacked by the vile-looking rat. When the attack didn't come, he moved slowly toward the opposite side of the other bed. Gardiner was not there.

"Mr. Gardiner?" he said. "Where the hell could he be?"

He opened the door to the bathroom to look in, but no sooner had he opened it than a large,

brown bat, mouth open, flew into his face.
Again he screamed. He slapped at the bat. He
tried to run from it, but all he could manage to
do was turn in circles. He tried to cover his face
with his arms and hands, and he felt the bat
snatching at his hair. He reached for the door,
but the bat was there again, fluttering in his
face. He turned and ran back to the bed from
which he had come. The bat had vanished.

"Mr. Gardiner," he shouted. "Where the hell
are you? Help!"

Then he heard the laugh, an insane-sounding
laugh, a cruel laugh. It was Gardiner's laugh, all
right, but it had a sinister ring about it that
Fishgall hadn't noticed before.

"Where are you?" he demanded.

"I'm right here, Fishguts," came the voice.

Then coming down from the lamp on the wall
above Fishgall's head was a monstrous black-
snake. Its face came even with his, and it looked
into his eyes, and it flicked its tongue in and out.
Fishgall opened his mouth to scream again, but
this time no sound came out. His eyes rolled
back in his head, the strength left his body, and
he passed out in a dead faint. In another moment the form of Vernon Gardiner appeared on
the other bed, sprawled out and shaking with
laughter.

Chapter Twenty-two

Jim Green flew into the Tulsa International Airport and rented a car, then headed east on Highway 51. It had been a few years since he had been home to eastern Oklahoma, but the landscape was immediately familiar, in spite of new housing and road construction, and he felt in place. He drove through Broken Arrow, Coweta, Wagoner, and Hulbert, and in Tahlequah, he stopped to eat at the Restaurant of the Cherokees.

He kept expecting to see familiar faces, but he didn't. He wasn't disappointed, however.

Had he run into relatives or old friends, they would have asked him his business, tried to delay him. He couldn't afford the delays, and he wouldn't be able to explain.

How could anyone who had not seen the carnage, not weighed the evidence, begin to believe the incredible tale he had to tell? He wondered if even the old man he had come back to Oklahoma to visit would believe him. How would he tell the tale, he wondered, and not sound ludicrous—or insane?

He left Tahlequah on Highway 10, driving along parallel to the scenic Illinois River. The river was low now, but he could still see evidence of recent flooding. *Some things never change,* he thought. He slowed as a pickup with a trailer load of canoes pulled onto the road ahead of him. The tourists were out on the river.

To his left a wall of sheer rock rose sharply, and at one point it seemed to lean out over the highway. He drove through Scraper, and soon the little engine of the rental car began to strain as it assaulted the steep hills to make the climb into Delaware County. He drove to Little Kansas and continued on where Highways 10 and 59 become the same for a stretch, and then he began to watch the side roads carefully.

Somewhere on this piece of highway was the turnoff he wanted. It had been years since he had been there. The old man could have moved since then. He might have died. Green didn't think so, though. For some reason, he felt confident that the old man was there, right now, this moment, awaiting his arrival.

Judith Ann walked into the youth shelter after double-checking the address on the card the policeman had given her. She was hungry again, but she was ashamed to go back to the other place for another free meal. She was afraid of the people in that place, too. *Bums and winos,* she thought. *They might cut my throat for my suitcase, or rape me or something.*

As she stepped into the building, she dropped the suitcase just inside the door. Her fingers ached from hauling it around. Suddenly self-conscious about her appearance, she made a futile attempt to brush unruly strands of hair back out of her face. A woman behind a desk looked up and smiled.

"Hi," she said. "Can I help you?"

Judith Ann dragged her feet over to the desk.

"Sit down," said the woman. "I'm Donna. You look beat. Can I get you a Coke?"

"Yes," said Judith Ann. "Please."

Donna went into an adjoining room and re-emerged a moment later with a cold can. She handed it to Judith Ann, then went back to her chair. Judith Ann sucked greedily at the can.

"Now, then," said Donna, her energy and

cheerfulness seeming unreal, even unrealistic, to Judith Ann, "what's your name?"

"Judith Ann Baylor."

"Okay, Judith Ann Baylor," said Donna, "how can I help you?"

"I ran away from home," said Judith Ann.

"Do you want to go back?" Donna asked her.

"I don't think they'll want me now," Judith Ann said. She paused a moment, then added, "I'm pregnant."

"Oh dear," said Donna. "Well, you know, I see lots of girls very much like you, and you'd be amazed at how happy their parents usually are to hear from them and to get them back home. Your parents just might surprise you."

"I don't know," said Judith Ann.

"Why did you leave home, Judith Ann?" Donna asked. "Can you tell me?"

"We had a fight," said Judith Ann, "and I wanted to go live with my father—my real dad."

"Oh, you have a stepfather?" Donna asked.

"Yeah," said Judith Ann. "Don."

"And they wouldn't let you go live with your father?"

"No. But he has a new wife too, and I guess they don't want me around either."

"What about Don?" Donna asked. "Does he want you around?"

"He says he does," Judith Ann said. "I mean, he did, before I left."

Robert J. Conley

"Would you like to call them, Judith Ann?" Donna asked.

Judith Ann sat silent for a moment, surprised at how she wanted to answer, surprised at what she had already said to this stranger.

"I don't know," she said. "I don't know what to say."

"Just tell them the truth," Donna said. "See what they have to say. Why don't you?"

Judith Ann didn't answer. She wondered who would answer the phone. What if it was Don? What could she say to him? What if she did tell him the truth? Would he scream at her? Call her a little slut? And what about her mother? Her mother would cry. She knew that.

She didn't want to make her mother cry, didn't think that she could stand to hear it. But Mother might be crying right now, worrying, wondering where Judith Ann might be, whether she was dead or alive. And what would she do if she didn't call? She couldn't just go back to walking the streets of Las Vegas. Girls who did that wound up being whores. She had heard of that happening. And then there was the baby. Sooner or later that was going to have to be reckoned with too. Did she really have a choice?

On a narrow, rocky, unpaved road winding through Ozark foothills deep in the woods of Delaware County, Oklahoma, a newly constructed one-room cabin stood off to one side of a modern four-bedroom house of the type known in those parts of the country as an Indian house, meaning that it had been built under a federally funded tribal housing project. The cabin had attached to it a front porch, the roof extending well over it. Hanging from the eaves around the porch were a variety of local plants in various stages of drying. The house and cabin were situated in a large, neatly mowed yard, giving the whole an anachronistic appearance there in the rustic environment. Inside the cabin, Jim Green sat talking to another Cherokee, a man perhaps in his late sixties, perhaps older. They talked in Cherokee.

"It's a strange tale you've told me, Grandson," the old man said.

"Yes," said Green. "I know."

"Do you really believe the old tale to be a true story?" the old man asked. "And do you really believe these things you've described have been done by *Untsaiyi*?"

"For a while I wasn't sure," Green said, "but there's nothing else I can believe. I've told you of the evidence."

The old man lit another cigarette. Green had noticed that he was like a chain smoker while he sat with company in his doctoring house. He had noticed also that the old man smoked cigarettes from a pack with its entire top ripped open. That meant that the cigarettes had all been removed from the pack, doctored, and then replaced. The old man took no chances, he thought. The old man expelled a cloud of smoke and stared into it.

"First of all," he said, "you'll need some protection for yourself and for your friends. Tonight we'll work on that."

When Fishgall had come to his senses again, hours after having passed out, or fainted, he wasn't sure which, he had been firmly convinced that the frightful animals that had menaced him in the motel room had been real. He couldn't figure out where they had come from or where they had gone, or, for that matter, what had become of his new boss, Mr. Vernon Gardiner, during the whole ordeal. But Gardiner had simply laughed at the tale the next day, and Fishgall had finally decided that it had all been nothing more than a bad drunk.

He had heard jokes all his life about drunks seeing pink elephants. Well, why not rats and bats and snakes? He shivered just remembering the experience. In the future, he resolved, he would buy a better quality of wine. Then there would be no more ghastly, drunken hallucinations. The situation with Gardiner was just too good to walk away from because of one bad batch of booze.

270

He still didn't know what his job was. He had to bathe regularly and wear clean clothes. He had explained a variety of gambling games to Gardiner, who remained to him a mysterious and somewhat frightening fellow, and often he had to read things to him. He gave thanks to the memory of his mother for having made him go to school, for Gardiner paid him well, and he had no expenses. He lived in Gardiner's room, and Gardiner paid the bill, bought his food and booze and clothes. What more could he want?

Brass was happy. His new identity was working out marvelously. The body of Vernon Gardiner was a pleasant enough one to be in, and the man's situation, which Brass had moved into, was comfortable. He had a fine motel room with a color television set, a more than adequate wardrobe, a big, luxurious car, and plenty of money. He also had Fishgall, and he had learned from him several of the games these modern gamblers played.

He had been able to either win a little or at least break even, so the money was holding out, but his mind was still on Big Bertha and her occasional million-dollar-or-more jackpot. He had begun again using his original tactic for spying on the computer room, but so far there had been no word of a time for the next big win.

Well, he was cozy, and he would wait, and

271

one day he would win it all. In the meantime, he would continue to spy, and he would play at other games, and now and then he would get drunk with Fishguts. He would be careful, though, in the future, not to tease Fishguts the way he had that first night he had gotten drunk, because that had nearly frightened the poor little man into leaving him, and he was handy to have around, at least for a little while longer.

Judith Ann held the telephone receiver to her ear, listening to the ring. *God,* she thought, *I hope Mom answers. Not Don. Please.* It rang again. *They're not home. They're not even home.* The next ring was interrupted by the sound of someone's lifting of the receiver on the other end.

"Hello?"

God it's Don.

Judith Ann sat on the edge of her chair gripping the receiver tightly and pressing it hard against her ear until it hurt.

"Hello?" Don said. "Who is this? Is anyone there? Hello."

"Don?" Judith Ann said, in her tiniest voice.

"Yeah. This is Don. Who—Judith Ann? Is that you? Oh my God. Elsa. Elsa, come here. Quick. Judith Ann, is that you?"

"It's me," she said.

"My God," Don said, "where are you? Elsa, it's Judith Ann."

"I'm in Las Vegas, Don," Judith Ann said.

"Las Vegas? Nevada?"

"Yeah."

"What are you doing there?" he said. "How did you get there?"

"I ran away, Don," said Judith Ann, and she was crying. "I'm sorry."

"Do you want to talk to your mother?" Don asked her. "She's right here."

"No."

Judith Ann shocked herself with her quick negative response to that question and the realization that somehow it was easier talking to Don just at that moment than it would be talking to her mother.

"No," she said. "Not now. Not yet. Don, I'm pregnant."

She heard no immediate response, and a sensation of panic raced through her body.

"Don, I'm pregnant," she said again. "And I want to come home. Can I?"

"Sure you can," said Don. "Of course you can. This is your home, and we want you here. Especially now. Okay? Do you have any money?"

"No."

"Then give me an address," he said, "and we'll come and get you."

"When?" she whined.

Robert J. Conley

Judith Ann felt her voice begin to crack, and tears began running freely from her eyes.

"Right now, baby," said Don. "We'll leave right now. Just tell me where to find you."

Chapter Twenty-three

Shelby picked Jim Green up in the Travelall at the Las Vegas airport and drove him back to the hotel, which was still serving as headquarters for the four hunters of the elusive monster known as Brass. Throughout the entire drive, Green remained silent about his trip. He wouldn't talk to Shelby alone about what he had learned in Oklahoma. He was saving that for a full meeting of the team back at the hotel. Shelby had to forcefully restrain himself in the busy city traffic from speeding and otherwise driving recklessly, so anxious was he to hear something, anything hopeful from Green.

Green, on the other hand, seemed amazingly calm, almost subdued, yet his features betrayed a renewed determination. What had begun with Green as academic curiosity had become total commitment. He was *Anagalisgi*. Lightning, and he was in pursuit of Brass. In his mind, it was Ancient Time once again on the face of the earth, and he had a heroic destiny to fulfill.

One image from his recent trip played and replayed itself inside his head: The old man had spent the first night with Green, preparing the medicine for the hunters' protection. The second night he had spent alone. Then he had returned to Green, and he had spoken with absolute conviction.

"I've talked to my helpers," he said, "and there's only one way."

It was that one way which Green now had the responsibility of explaining to his partners, and it was imperative that he convince them that it was, in fact, the only way.

"We'll never find him," said Green. "We have no idea what shape he might be in at any given moment, and even if we did figure out what he looks like, he'd just change into something else before we could act."

"We can't just give up," said Kay.

"No," Green said. "Of course we can't, but

what we have to do is this. We can't find him, so we have to make him come to us."

"Great," said Chase. "Just how the hell do you propose that we do that?"

"Why did Brass come to Vegas in the first place?" Green asked.

"For the gambling," said Shelby. "Hell. We all know that."

"Right," said Green. "Do you remember the original story?"

"Yeah. Sure," Shelby said.

"He was a gambler," said Kay.

"He's the inventor of a specific gambling game," said Green. "One that not only Cherokees, but just about all southeastern Indians were fanatical about for centuries. His passion, his real passion, is *gatayusti*."

"Got a what?" said Chase.

"*Gatayusti* is the Cherokee name for the stone and stick game," said Green. "The Creeks call it *chunkey*."

"That's easier to say," said Chase.

"As far as I know, nobody plays it anymore," Green said. "Well, we've got to give Brass the opportunity. It's the only chance we've got."

"So what do we do?" asked Chase. "Open a chunkey casino?"

"Almost," Green said enthusiastically. "We'll need Shelby's work crew, and we'll need the cooperation of the U.S. government, probably the Pentagon."

"We've got that," said Shelby. "No problem. We've got Niles. So what's the plan?"

"We have to select a spot on the beach," said Green. "We have to put him right back the way he was. The government's going to have to condemn this place we select, fence it off, block it somehow to keep people out, from the beach and from the ocean."

"That can be done," said Shelby.

"Then we have to construct a chunkey yard," Green continued, "and that's the thing that's going to lure him into our trap."

"But how the hell do we spear him and pin him down?" asked Chase.

"I think we'll have to find a way to shoot the pole," Green said. "Shelby? You're the engineer. It's got to hit him before he knows it's coming. We can't give him time to do his thing, you know, change into something else and fly away or something like that."

"Yeah," said Shelby. "I got you. Yeah. I think we can do that. We can use a telephone pole or something like that. Is that too big?"

"I don't think so," Green said.

"Well," Shelby said, Green's excitement beginning to grip him too, "we'll check it against the size of the one we ripped up, the original one. Then we sharpen it on one end, like a giant pencil. Right? We fit a length of pipe to it, seal the pipe at some point, bury its end in cement to stabilize it, and we've got ourselves a basic, old-fashioned cannon. We use gunpowder and a fuse, and, hell yes, we can shoot the damn pole."

"Hell's bells," said Chase. "If anyone had ever told me I'd be taking part in a serious discussion of a plan to shoot somebody with a goddamned telephone pole, I'd have told him he was nuts. Pure and simple. How the hell do you aim the damn thing?"

"You don't," said Green. "You plan the trajectory and construct the cannon along with the chunkey yard. Then it's up to me to get Brass into just the right position for the shot."

"What do you mean it's up to you?" said Kay. "Just what are you going to be doing?"

"I'm going to be gambling with him," said Green. "Playing chunkey."

The other three all looked at Green in disbelief. He shrugged.

"Someone's got to do it," he said. "Any of you know how to play the game?"

There was a pause, a moment of silence, broken at last by Shelby.

"It could work," he said.

"Yeah," said Chase, still skeptical. "Sure. So we build all this shit back out on the coast. Okay. How do we tell him about it?"

"Television," said Green. "TV advertising."

Chase took the last Marlboro out of his crumpled pack. It was bent and twisted, but the paper wasn't broken anywhere.

"If this thing hadn't already made me crazy," he said, "I'd think I was going nuts."

There was still no word from the computers on Big Bertha, and Brass was becoming more irritable with each passing day. He had lost heavily at craps, and he had never been a good loser. It had taken all his willpower to make him quit the game, but he knew that he couldn't allow himself to run out of money again. He needed money for the room, for food, for gasoline, and for wine. He needed it to keep Fishguts on the string, but most of all, he needed it for the day Big Bertha would be scheduled once again to belch forth millions.

He was growing weary of the role of the cockroach, tired of watching out for the big feet while making the long journey to the wire behind Big Bertha, and sick of the long crawl along the length of wire in the dark. But most of all, he was bored from sitting for hours in the dark shadows and listening to the stupid, boring men in the computer room, waiting, endlessly waiting, for the announcement that could at once make him a millionaire and secure for him his sweet revenge for having been robbed of it all the last time.

Shelby pulled the Travelall with his three partners in it off the road and headed it toward the ocean. Up ahead, the land seemed to stop abruptly, as if they had suddenly arrived at the western edge of the world. There was a long drop straight down to a sandy beach and the waves, which rolled in endlessly from the vast expanse of sea. Shelby shut off the ignition, and they all got out and walked to the edge of the precipice.

"How's this look, Jim?" said Shelby.

"It looks good to me," Green said. "Can you build the chunkey yard right up here?"

"Yeah," Shelby said. "Sure."

"How and where are you going to shoot the bastard?" Chase asked.

"I thought we'd play the game with our backs to the ocean," said Green. "Then the shot could come from the east, carrying him off into the water."

"No," said Shelby. "That's no good. The trajectory would carry him out into the ocean, all right, but it would never carry him all the way down to the bottom with the right angle and force to plant the pole."

"What, then?" Green asked.

"I've been figuring on this," Shelby said. "In

281

order to plant him right, to make it work, to get him down there the way he was before, the pole, with him impaled on it, needs to drop almost straight down into the water. The only way to get that angle is to fire the damn thing almost straight up."

"Then how the hell do you hit him?" said Chase.

"I dig a hole," said Shelby, "right over here, deeper than the length of the pole, a hole like a well just off to the side of the chunkey yard. Down at the bottom of the well, we set the cannon in cement at an angle to give us the proper trajectory."

"Same question," said Chase. "How do you hit him?"

"You'd have to get him to lean over and look right down into the well," said Kay.

"I can do that," Green said.

"And then we shoot," said Shelby.

"How you going to set that thing off?" Chase asked, taking out a cigarette. "With a fuse? It's got to be a quick shot."

"Electronic detonator," said Shelby. "Instantaneous."

"Joe," said Kay, "if you dig a hole like a well straight down here, how are you going to work down there at the bottom of the hole to set the pipe in cement and all that stuff?"

"We'll tunnel in from down on the beach,"

Shelby said. "Make a shaft to connect up with the bottom of the well. Hell, don't worry about it. I know what I'm doing."

Chase managed to get his Marlboro lit in spite of the slight breeze that blew in from the ocean. He exhaled, and the smoke quickly vanished in the wind.

"Okay," he said, "we build all this stuff. We get Green here on TV with his game. Brass sees it, we hope, and hurries on down here to play the game. Green somehow gets him to lean over the hole and, blooey, we blast him. You've got it all engineered so that the pole goes through Brass just enough to carry him along with it in a high arc, then down into the water and pin him to the ocean floor. Have I got it all right?"

"That's about the size of it," said Shelby.

"And then," added Kay, "the Army comes in to seal off the beach."

"Right," said Shelby.

"If it works," said Kay.

"It's got to," said Shelby. He put an arm around Kay's shoulder and hugged her to his side. Then he looked at Chase and at Jim Green.

"Let's get to work," he said.

The graders leveled off the land for the playing field three feet lower than the land surrounding it. It was rectangular, about one hundred feet long and twelve feet wide, and was situated with one end up near the drop-off to the beach below. Between the end of the playing field and the drop-off was a space of about six feet. The rectangular playing field was bordered by a two-foot-high mound of earth with an opening left, like a gateway, into the field at each end.

The chunkey yard itself, the actual playing field, was finished off with a smooth layer of hard-packed sand. A few feet to the south, Shelby's "well" was dug, and down below on the beach, a tunnel was cut into the cliff to intersect with the well. The cement slab was poured into the bottom of the well, and the modified pipe, or improvised cannon, was set in at the proper angle, the trajectory having been carefully plotted.

Several poles having been milled to specifications were brought in to the site. A carefully selected stone was ground and polished to make a perfectly symmetrical wheel with a six-inch diameter and a thickness of about an inch. It had a polished concavity on either side. Several straight, eight-foot-long hickory sticks were prepared, much like spears or long arrows, and greased with bear oil. All of this had been done according to Jim Green's instructions.

At an assumed safe distance down the beach, still up on the cliff, a tower was constructed overlooking the yard and the ocean, and when all was prepared, the extra wooden missiles, which had been treated with creosote for longer life in the water, were test fired, set off from the tower by Joe Shelby with an electronic remote control switch. Chase sat beside him, watching through a pair of high-power binoculars. The trajectory was correct. Each of the test poles planted itself firmly in the floor of the ocean.

While all of this was going on, Jim Green had returned to his office at the university to do some research. He had remembered enough detail to give Shelby instructions for setting up the chunkey yard and preparing the stone wheel and the throwing sticks, but he had never before actually played the *gatayusti*, or *chunkey*, game, had never even seen it played.

He got out all the books he could find on the cultures of the southeastern American Indians, quickly discarded all those with no references to the game, then settled down with the remainder. Nowhere could he find all the necessary information on the way the game had been played by the Cherokees.

He found a bit in one source about how the Cherokees scored the game, in another he found the length of the Choctaw throwing sticks, in yet another there were more specific scoring details from the Chickasaws, and in a final source, the dimensions of the Choctaw playing field. *Damn*, he thought. He would have to play it by ear, just make up his own rules based on this hodgepodge of information and hope for the best. He could try to get away with telling Brass, if he should be challenged, that the rules had changed over the centuries.

Or, he thought, he could allow Brass to set the rules. After all, he recalled, Brass was some kind of supernatural creature. He was not a Cherokee. Presumably he had played in Ancient Time with anyone he could grab hold of, regardless of tribe.

Green knew that he would have to play the game for a while before he would be able to maneuver Brass into the necessary position for the kill—so to speak. During that time, he would have to make it look good. He would have to be at least an acceptable *gatayusti* player, and that was not going to be easy. He was going to be facing the expert, the man, or superman, who had invented the game. He got all he could from the books, then headed back to the beach. He would need some practice.

In the casino's computer room, one man sat with his feet propped up on a table, his arms folded behind his head. Another sat watching a monitor.

"Hey, Wilkins," said the one with his feet up, "you want to split the cost of a pizza with me? I'll call."

"Sure, Rudy," Wilkins said.

Rudy got up to make the phone call. He gave his name and instructions on how to find the computer room in the casino, and he asked for the price.

"Oh, yeah," he said. "Just a minute. Hey, Wilkie. What kind you like?"

"Garbage can," said Wilkins.

"One of them kind with everything on it," said Rudy back into the phone. "You know. Supreme. Yeah. Whatever. Large. Okay. Thanks."

He hung up the phone and went back to his chair, resuming his previous position.

"Be about a half an hour," he said. "They must be busy tonight."

"Okay," Wilkins said.

They sat in silence for another ten minutes. Then Rudy got up again.

"Got to take a piss," he said. "Let me back in when I knock."

"Okay," said Wilkins. "Hey. Wait a minute."

"What?" asked Rudy.

"Looky here," Wilkins said. "Big Bertha's due to pay off again."

"The big one?"

"Five mil."

"When?"

"One week from tonight," said Wilkins. "Sometime between eight and ten."

"Hot damn," said Rudy, and he went on out of the room.

On a wire just inside a hole in the wall peering out into the room, a cockroach watched and listened.

Chapter Twenty-four

It had seemed like a long wait to Brass, almost too long, but now he was overjoyed. He knew that this time he would be able to make it work. He had a form in which he was perfectly at home. He had money, and he had the cards he would need to show the men in the back room. All of his patience had at last paid off.

On the specially prepared beach, patience was still wearing thin. The construction had actually gone pretty smoothly and pretty fast, but the four monster chasers were so conscious of the fact that Brass was at large, out there some-where, doing who knows what and to whom, that the process seemed almost interminable. It seemed that way to everyone except Jim Green.

Green was utterly, almost painfully, con-scious of the task he had assigned to himself, or rather, the task that had been thrust upon him. He had a sense that he had never really had a choice. The old man at home had told him what to do, and he was *Anagalisgi*. But he needed time to practice. He was going to be facing Brass.

He worked every day, all day, until Shelby and the others thought that he would wear him-self out. Still he practiced. He felt like a college boy getting ready to step into the ring with Mu-hammed Ali, or trying to run a football past Jim Thorpe, or pitch a baseball past Babe Ruth, or— No. There were no analogies strong enough to express the feeling.

He needed all the practice he could get, but at the same time, he realized that they needed to attract Brass to the trap soon. If at all possi-ble, they needed to get him before he caused any more harm to anyone else.

At last, Jim Green had discarded his contem-porary clothing and donned buckskin leggings with breechclout and moccasins. On his head he wore a colorful cloth turban, heavily decorated with peacock and pheasant feathers. He had beaded armbands, and across his otherwise bare chest was a broad band that supported the large, beaded bandolier bag that was hanging on his right hip. The bag was stuffed with a variety of beaded items and shells.

"You look handsome, Jim," said Kay.

"Let's just hope it does the trick," Green said.

The work crew had at last finished its job and had been sent away, Shelby was below in the shaft making last-minute checks of the powder charge and the fuse, and Chase was surveying the landscape from the tower.

"It's got to," said Kay. "It's just got to."

"Well," said Green, "I'd best keep myself in shape. Can't just stand around here."

He picked up the chunkey stone in his left hand, cupping it down at his side. In his right hand he held a throwing stick. He took two steps and heaved the stone, with a motion much like that used in pitching a bowling ball, sending it rolling down the length of the chunkey yard on the hard-packed sand. Almost as soon as he'd released the stone, he took aim and sent the stick flying after it.

He'd had to estimate the distance the stone would roll and throw the stick at his estimated target. With the stone still rolling and the stick in the air, Green ran after them in the sand. When the stone stopped rolling and fell over on its side, Green's stick was a good five feet away from it. He stopped running and stood with his hands on his hips, staring at them.

"I'll have to do better than that against the champ," he said.

He picked up the stone and the stick and started back for the end of the field to try again. A car had just turned off the highway and was driving toward them, leaving a cloud of dust in its wake.

"Who's that coming?" Green asked.

"Looks like your TV crew," said Kay. "Are you ready to be a star?"

Brass, in the guise of Vernon Gardiner, lay back on the bed in his motel room. The television was on and tuned to *Wheel of Fortune*, his favorite show. He held a glass of red wine in his right hand. On the other bed, Fishgall slept, having already overindulged in the beverage. The show stopped for a commercial break, and Brass drained his glass, then got up to refill it from a jug that stood on the table.

Behind him he could hear the latest Dr Pepper jingle rasping out its message, but he wasn't paying attention to that. He was thinking about the fortune he was about to win from Big Bertha, and how the wild celebration at the casino was even better than the stuff on TV, even *Wheel of Fortune*.

When he had his millions, he thought, maybe he could get on that show. He vaguely heard from over his shoulder the announcement of a news break. He wasn't interested in that, but when the newsman started to speak, the television suddenly had the full attention of Brass again.

"Out on a lonely stretch of beach in southern California," said the newsman, "a Cherokee Indian is trying to revive a bit of his culture that was lost long ago. The gambling game known as *chunkey* hasn't been played for hundreds of years, but James Green, a professor of American Indian Studies, has constructed a new playing field, or *chunkey* yard, as he calls it, and he's getting in practice."

Brass had put down his wineglass and the jug and turned back to face the television set. The newsman's voice was coming out over video-taped footage of Jim Green in his new chunkey yard. Brass could scarcely believe what he was seeing and hearing. This was not just something of the old world which he remembered, which he knew so well, which he had feared had vanished utterly, this was his game!

"We asked Professor Green," the newsman continued, "who he expected to find to play this game with him, and he responded, 'You never know who might come along.' Chunkey, anyone?"

Brass stood stunned for a moment, then he

whirled upon the unsuspecting sleeper, swatting him vigorously across the rump.

"Fishguts," he roared. "Fishguts, wake up. I need you."

Fishgall yelped from the rude awakening, then sat up and rubbed his eyes.

"What? What?" he said, with considerable whine in his voice.

"Fishguts," said Brass, "there was a story on the TV set."

"What story?" Fishgall whimpered.

"About chunkey," Brass said. "My game! There's a chunkey yard somewhere. Find it for me, Fishguts. Hurry. Find it."

"How am I supposed to find this— Whatever it is?" Fishgall said. "I didn't hear the story, and I don't even know what it is you're talking about."

Brass grabbed Fishgall's shirtfront in both his hands and lifted the poor little man up from the bed. His own face almost touching Fishgall's, he snarled.

"Find it, Fishguts," he said, "or I'll kill you."

Big Bertha and her millions were suddenly and completely gone from the mind of Brass.

Shelby was in the tower with Chase when they saw General Niles driving toward them. Chase climbed down to meet the general, leaving Shelby up above with the glasses. Niles didn't bother getting out of his car or shutting off his engine. He rolled down the window as Chase walked toward him.

"Chase," he said, "we just got a phone call from the Vegas police. An unidentified male phoned the TV station your newsbreak spot was running on. He asked them for directions to the new chunkey yard. They told him how to get here, then called the police, the way they were instructed to do. The police called us. It sounds like your plan may be working. Good luck."

The general rolled up his window, turned his car around, and drove back to the highway. Chase ran back to the tower and called up to Shelby.

"He's on the way, Joe," he shouted. "Come on."

Shelby climbed down from the tower and ran with Chase over to the playing field.

"Jim. Jim," said Shelby. "It looks like he's on the way. Is everything ready here?"

"My bets are in the bag," said Green. "The sticks and the stone are right here. I wish I had more time to practice, that's all. What about down below?"

"I've checked it all out personally, Jim," said Shelby. "We're ready to roll. As soon as you get him to lean over that hole, we fire."

"There'll only be one chance," said Green. "Make it count."

"It will take him awhile to drive here from Vegas," said Kay. "We still have some time."

"If he drives," said Shelby. "How long does it take a bird to fly from Vegas to here?"

"We'd better get into position right away and be ready," said Chase.

"Just one thing before we do," said Green. He reached into his bandolier bag and pulled out a pack of Marlboros with the entire top torn open. "I want you all to smoke with me," he said. "You too, Mrs. Shelby."

"What?" said Chase.

"This is renewed tobacco," said Green. "It was prepared just for us. To help protect us from Brass. Smoke all over this field, down below in the shaft, and over at the tower. Get the smoke all over yourselves, too."

He handed a cigarette to each of the other three and took one for himself. Chase pulled a lighter out of his pocket.

"At least he uses the right brand," he said.

"Don't light it with that," said Green. "Use these."

He handed each of them a wooden kitchen match to use to light their smokes.

Brass saw the chunkey yard from the highway.

"Pull over," he shouted.

Fishgall braked and pulled the Lincoln off the road. Brass was out of the car before it had made its backward lurch and settled down to a full stop.

"Wait here for me, Fishguts," said Brass. "I'll be back, and I'll be rich."

North of the chunkey yard and still up on the ledge was a pile of large boulders. Brass headed for them. When he came out the other side, he was no longer Vernon Gardiner. He was Brass. He was naked, except for a loincloth around his middle.

"Goddamn, Shelby," said Chase. "Look!"

Up in the tower Chase handed the field glasses to Joe Shelby.

"Over toward those rocks over there," he said.

Shelby found the incredible figure of Brass.

"It's worked," he said. "That's him. It's got to be him."

He handed the glasses to Kay.

"Take a good look, babe," he said, "and let's all hope we never see the son of a bitch again."

"Oh my God," said Kay, looking at Brass through the glasses.

She handed them back to Chase.

"All right," said Shelby. "Don't take your eyes off him again. When you see him lean over that pole, give me the word."

Chapter Twenty-five

Green saw the naked figure loping toward him. It looked like an Indian, he thought, sort of. The man, if man he was, was huge. His skin was dark, and his black hair was chopped off just below his ears. As he came closer, Green could see the muscles ripple with each stride. The figure was solid, thick, hard looking. As it came even closer, he could see the horrible scar on the stomach. Green felt his heart rate increase. *This is Brass*, he thought. *Untsaiyi. He's real, and he's alive!* He held himself erect, took a long,

deep breath, and did his best to hide his awe—
and his fear.

"Hello, little man," said Brass, stopping just a
few feet in front of Green. "What language do
you talk?"

"I talk Cherokee, and I talk English," said
Green.

"Well, then," said Brass, "we'll talk Cherokee.
English is too ugly. You look lonesome here
with your brand-new *gatayusti* yard. Can you
play?"

"Of course I can play," said Green. "If I have
someone to play with. Why else would I have
this place?"

"Well, then," said Brass, "let's play."

"Why should I play with you?" Green said,
amazed at his own boldness. "You're practically
naked. What could you bet against the things I
have?"

"What do you have?" Brass asked.

Green pulled the bandolier bag off his shoulder and poured the contents out onto the
ground. Then he took the turban off his head
and dropped it beside the other stuff. He slung
the bag back over his shoulder.

"All these things," he said. "And more. Come
back when you have something to put up
against these."

Brass stepped in closer to Green. He stood

over the pile of items Green had made and looked down at them. They were beautiful things, he thought, the kind of things he had thought were gone from the world for good. He wanted them, but he didn't know if this man would be willing to take his bet. He decided that boldness was the best course of action, and he extended his left arm, its big fist clenched.

"I have this," he said. He opened the fist to reveal a wad of bills, twenties, fifties, hundreds. "Do we play?"

"All of that," said Green, "against all of this. We play to twelve."

"Agreed," said Brass.

Brass threw his money to the ground beside Green's stake.

"Choose a stick," said Green.

Brass picked up each of the sticks and hefted them. He sighted down their lengths, then settled on one.

"This is good," he said. "It's your yard. Roll the wheel."

Green took his time in selecting a stick, then picked up the stone wheel. He stepped up to the opening in the mound that bordered the playing field, looked out over the length of the smooth sand, took two steps, and flung the stone. Before he had drawn back his hand to toss his stick after it, Brass had let fly his stick and was already running.

Damn, thought Green. It didn't seem possible. He threw his stick and ran. Brass was standing beside the stone wheel as it lay over on its side. His stick was two inches from the wheel. Green's was three feet away.

"Ha!" said Brass. "I get one. You got none. I thought you said you could play this game."

"My foot slipped," Green said. "Let's go back."

Green picked up his stick, and Brass picked up his and the stone. They walked together back to the end of the field.

"Are you ready, little friend?" Brass asked.

"Yes," said Green.

Brass tossed the stone with an easy flick of his wrist and sent his stick after it almost at the same time. Green flung his stick with all his strength and ran. The result was the same as the last time.

"Two for me," said Brass. "None for you. Pretty soon I'll have all your pretty things there. You roll."

They played again, and this time Green's stick came close enough for a point, but Brass's stick was touching the stone.

"Now I get two for that one," said Brass. "Four for me and one for you."

At least I got one, thought Green as he picked up the stone and his stick.

"You don't have twelve yet," he said boldly.

"But I will," said Brass, "soon."

And soon Brass did have twelve, and Green had only the one. Brass scooped up all the beaded items from the ground. He put armbands on his arms and necklaces around his neck. He wrapped the turban around his head.

"How do I look?" he said, a broad grin on his wide face. When Green didn't answer, he spoke again. "Let's play another game. You might get lucky and win all this back. What else do you have to bet?"

Green tossed down the bandolier bag. He pulled the armbands off his arms and tossed them down with it. He took off his moccasins and his leggings, leaving him in just the breechclout, and he dropped them onto the new pile of goods.

"All that," he said.

"Against what?" asked Brass.

"Against my own things that you won from me," Green said.

"Agreed," said Brass, and they played again. Green made four points in the second game to Brass's winning twelve. He was getting a little better, but he was also getting tired. Brass, on the other hand, seemed to be getting better and livelier the more he played. Green decided that there could only be one more game. He had to bet it all on the next one. He sat on the ground panting while Brass pulled on the leggings and the moccasins. The monster was laughing.

302

"Who's naked now?" he asked.

"Play again," said Green.

"You don't have anything to bet," said Brass. "Why should I play you again?"

"I have this place," said Green, "this *gatayusti* yard, and the stone and the sticks. I'll bet it against all the things you have, the things you won from me and your money. Is it a bet?"

"Yes," said Brass, "and when you lose, you have to get out. You have to go just as you are, and go naked among the mean, ugly pale people out there. Let's play."

Brass picked up the pace of the game and laughed at Green trying to keep up. Once, with the score nine to two in Brass's favor, Green fell down on his face in the sand while running after the toss. Brass laughed so hard that he, too, fell down, but on his backside rather than on his face. Soon he had won the game, and Green could barely stand.

"Now get out," said Brass. "This is my place now."

"Wait," said Green. "You have to give me a chance to win my things back."

"But you don't have any bet," said Brass.

"I have a treasure," said Green, "which I've hidden away."

"Where is it?" Brass said.

"It's buried," said Green.

"Where?"

"Will you play me for it?" Green asked.

"Let me see it first," said Brass.

"All right," said Green. "It's right over here."
He walked to Shelby's well and pointed down
the hole. "It's hidden down there," he said.

Chase could see Green indicating the hole to
Brass. Then he saw Brass move toward it and
hesitate.

"Get ready," he said to Shelby.

Shelby tensed. Chase watched through the
glasses as Brass dropped to his knees beside the
hole, then leaned forward, catching himself on
his hands, one on each side of the hole, in preparation for looking down for the treasure, his
belly and chest directly above the sharpened
missile.

"Now," he said.

It was dark inside the hole. He couldn't see a
treasure. He couldn't see anything but darkness. No. There was a little light coming into
the bottom of the hole from somewhere, and it
was gleaming on something. The treasure!

Then there was a flash deep down in the hole,
a blinding flash, and a roar came with it that
was deafening, and almost as soon as he saw
the flash, heard the roar, he felt the thing driving through his guts, felt himself flying upward.
He roared in pain and anger, and his roar filled

the welkin over the land and the sea.

Jim Green had fallen to the earth and covered his head with his arms against the blast, and he felt the ground shake, and he felt the vibrations in the air from the bellowing of Brass. He rolled over and looked up, and he could see the great, long pole shooting straight up overhead, and suddenly he saw impaled on it a giant alligator, lashing at the air with its long tail. The roaring continued, but the shape changed again right before Green's eyes. It was a bear with the pole through its guts, and it roared and slapped at the pole with its paws.

Then the pole reached the zenith of its trajectory, and it began to curve out over the ocean, and Green saw in rapid succession on the pole as it zoomed toward the waiting water below, a dog, a puma, and a monstrous snake, writhing and wrapping itself about the pole. Then, with a final resounding and agonized scream, Brass was himself again, and he splashed on his back into the ocean. The pole drove its way to the bottom and deep into the ocean floor.

Up above, Green beside the playing field and the Shelbys and Chase in the tower saw the waters rise to a tremendous height, saw sand and debris from the disturbed ocean floor spread beneath the surface of the water in a dark cloud, saw the surface begin at last to calm, and saw the end of the pole sticking several feet out of

305

the water when all had finally settled. The pole still vibrated a little from its impact with the ocean floor. Up in the tower, Kay Shelby saw a movement in the sky and turned her head.

"Look," she said.

Two old black crows swooped by the tower and circled out over the pole. Then they settled on its end. The pole was suddenly shaken violently from down below, and the crows began to scream.

Ka, ka, ka.

Shelby, Kay, and Chase climbed down from the tower and hurried over to meet Green there beside the field.

"You all right?" asked Shelby.

"Yeah," said Green. "I'm okay."

"It's over," said Kay. "Isn't it?"

Green looked at her and smiled.

"It's over," he said.

"I'll go notify General Niles to move in with the Army and close off this area," said Chase.

"You know," said Green, "if I'd had a month to get in shape, I think I could have beat him."

Epilogue

It had been more than two years since Judith
Ann had seen John Brass, since the day he had
gone out to win the million dollars from Big
Bertha and make them rich and had never come
back, two years since she had seen the man who
was the father of her son. Her mother and Don
had been good to her. They hadn't lectured her
on morality, hadn't even asked too many questions. They had asked her what she wanted to
do about the baby, and when she had said that
she wanted to have it and to keep it, they had
not argued.

Robert J. Conley

They had agreed and said that they were pleased and were proud of her. They had said that their home was her home and would be the home of the baby too, for as long as Judith Ann wanted it that way. So she had stayed, and she had delivered little Johnny, and now he was eighteen months old.

She had nursed him. No bottles and formulas for her baby. He was healthy and handsome, and she loved him. But at eighteen months, he had started to be bothersome. Judith Ann wanted to go out and have fun, and her mother wouldn't allow her often enough to go out and leave little Johnny at home with her. He was beginning to be a bit of a burden to Judith Ann. God, she thought. She was only eighteen years old. She deserved a little fun too.

It was a Friday evening, and Judith Ann and Johnny were at home alone. Don and her mother had gone to a party at Don's boss's house. There was nothing good to watch on television, so Judith Ann had put a CD in the player—hard rock. She was bored. Johnny toddled over to the stereo and reached toward where he had seen her put the shiny disc. Judith Ann jumped up and ran to stop him.

"No," she said, and she slapped his hand. He started to cry as she turned her back on him to walk back to the couch. Then the crying stopped. Judith Ann heard something like a screech or a yowl, and she felt sharp claws dig deep into the back of her calf. She screamed and kicked. The cat was flung off her leg and across the room, and Judith Ann ran into the next room and shut the door.

She looked at her leg. The blood was running freely down onto her foot. She winced in pain, then she realized that she had left Johnny behind. She didn't know where the cat had come from. She and her parents had no pets. She slowly opened the door and peeked back into the room. The rock music was still blaring. She saw no cat. Johnny was sitting in the middle of the floor, a happy smile on his face.

He writhed in pain and felt the sharp sand and the shells and pebbles bite into his back. The long pole was all the way through his guts and had him pinned down securely to the ocean floor. The pain in his innards was seething. He felt like there was a fire in his belly.

He knew though that the pain would slowly subside, and there would come a time when out of sheer boredom, he would actually miss it, but for now it put him in a rage, a rage about which he could do nothing. He could thrash around and howl, but it would do no good. It would only increase the pain and make the hated crows up above shriek their horrible *ka ka*s at him.

Robert J. Conley

A big fish floated by just over his face, and he hated it for it was free. He took a swing at it with his right arm, and the sudden motion tore at his fresh wound. He roared out in his pain, and the roar became a loud gargle, and the bubbles rose fast toward the surface.

He wished that he could rise so easily and escape this wet and slimy prison. He knew that he could not. He had not been able to the first time. Something unknown had rescued him that time. Perhaps it would again. How long must he wait? Would the world be all changed again? he wondered.

He knew from painful experience that a time would come when he would be able to sleep, not to sleep exactly, but to drift off into a kind of semiconsciousness, become nearly oblivious to his otherwise unendurable situation. He longed for that time, even as he longed for rescue or escape.

He thought about Judith Ann, and he thought about the *gatayusti* yard. He thought of the rich treasures he had almost had in his grasp, and the tears welled up behind his eyes, and they rolled out onto his cheeks where they were drawn away to mingle with the endless salt water around him.

Cold Blue Midnight

Ed Gorman

In Indiana the condemned die at midnight—killers like Peter Tapley, a twisted man who lives in his mother's shadow and takes his hatred out on trusting young women. Six years after Tapley's execution, his ex-wife Jill is trying to live down his crimes. But somewhere in the chilly nights someone won't let her forget. Someone who still blames her for her husband's hideous deeds. Someone who plans to make her pay . . . in blood.

___4417-X $4.99 US/$5.99 CAN

ROUGH BEAST
GARY GOSHGARIAN

"[Treads] territory staked out by John Saul and Dean Koontz...a solid and suspenseful cautionary tale."

—*Publishers Weekly*

A genocidal experiment conducted by the government goes horribly wrong, with tragic and terrifying results for the Hazzards, a normal, unsuspecting family in a small Massachusetts town. Every day, their son gradually becomes more of a feral, uncontrollable, and very dangerous...thing. The government is determined to do whatever is necessary to eliminate the evidence of their dark secret and protect the town...but it is already too late. The beast is loose!

_4152-9 $4.99 US/$5.99 CAN

HUNGRY EYES

BARRY HOFFMAN

The eyes are always watching. She can feel them as she huddles there, naked, vulnerable, in an iron cage in a twisted man's basement. Someday she will be the one with the power, the need to close the eyes. And she'll close them all.

___4449-8 $4.99 US/$5.99 CAN

Dorchester Publishing Co., Inc.
P.O. Box 6640
Wayne, PA 19087-8640

Please add $1.75 for shipping and handling for the first book and $.50 for each book thereafter. NY, NYC, and PA residents, please add appropriate sales tax. No cash, stamps, or C.O.D.s. All orders shipped within 6 weeks via postal service book rate. Canadian orders require $2.00 extra postage and must be paid in U.S. dollars through a U.S. banking facility.

Name_____
Address_____
City_____State_____Zip_____
I have enclosed $_____ in payment for the checked book(s).
Payment <u>must</u> accompany all orders. ☐ Please send a free catalog.

Elizabeth Massie

Sineater

According to legend, the sineater is a dark and mysterious figure of the night, condemned to live alone in the woods, who devours food from the chests of the dead to absorb their sins into his own soul. To look upon the face of the sineater is to see the face of all the evil he has eaten. But in a small Virginia town, the order is broken. With the violated taboo comes a rash of horrifying events. But does the evil emanate from the sineater...or from an even darker force?

___4407-2 $5.99 US/$6.99 CAN

DRAWN TO THE GRAVE — MARY ANN MITCHELL

"A tight, taut dark fantasy with surprising plot twists and a lot of spooky atmosphere."
—Ed Gorman

Beverly thinks that she has found something special with Carl, until she realizes that he has stolen from her. But he doesn't just steal her money and her property—he steals her very life. Suddenly she is helpless and alone, able only to watch in growing despair as her flesh begins to decay and each day transforms her more and more into a corpse—a corpse without the release of death.

But Beverly is not truly alone, for Carl is always nearby, watching her and waiting. He knows that soon he will need another unknowing victim, another beautiful woman he can seduce...and destroy. And when lovely young Megan walks into his web, he knows he has found his next lover. For what can possibly go wrong with his plan, a plan he has practiced to perfection so many times before?

___4290-8 $4.99 US/$5.99 CAN

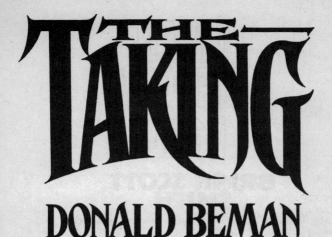

THE TAKING

DONALD BEMAN

What could Sean McDonald possibly have done to deserve what is happening to him? He was a happy man with a beautiful family, a fine job, good friends and dreams of becoming a writer. Now bit by bit, his life is crumbling. Everything and everyone he values is disappearing. Or is it being taken from him? Someone or something is determined to break Sean, to crush his mind and spirit. A malicious, evil force is driving him to the very brink of insanity. But why him?

_4202-9 $4.99 US/$5.99 CAN

Dorchester Publishing Co., Inc.
P.O. Box 6640
Wayne, PA 19087-8640

Please add $1.75 for shipping and handling for the first book and $.50 for each book thereafter. NY, NYC, and PA residents, please add appropriate sales tax. No cash, stamps, or C.O.D.s. All orders shipped within 6 weeks via postal service book rate. Canadian orders require $2.00 extra postage and must be paid in U.S. dollars through a U.S. banking facility.

Name_____
Address_____
City_____State_____Zip_____
I have enclosed $_____ in payment for the checked book(s).
Payment <u>must</u> accompany all orders. ☐ Please send a free catalog.

WHEN SHADOWS FALL

BRIAN SCOTT SMITH

Martin doesn't believe his aunt's death is an accident, and he and a couple of buddies are determined to find the truth. But when he starts sneaking around the house of his aunt's new "friends," he never expects to witness a blood-drenched satanic ritual. But he does see it, and more important, the witches see him!

Suddenly Martin is in a horrifying race for his life. He has to stop the witches before they stop him for good. And he has to do it before Halloween night, the night of the final sacrifice, the night when the demons of hell will be unleashed on the Earth, the night when shadows fall.

___4313-0 $4.99 US/$5.99 CAN

EVIL INTENT

BERNARD TAYLOR

"Move over, Stephen King!"
—*New York Daily News*

John Callow hates the people of Valley Green. For years, Callow has waited while the townsfolk spurn him, insult him, cheat him. But with an ancient curse ripped from the bowels of hell, he'll visit misery on everyone who has ever slighted him. Death by grisly death, his neighbors will fall victim to a plague of ghastly suffering. And Callow's grim reaping will be stopped by neither heavenly prayer nor earthly weapon—only by an infernal power born in the same wicked domain as his evil intent.

__3904-4 $4.99